The Pool
A Novella

KT Ashely

The Pool
First edition

ISBN 978-0692459560
ISBN 0692459561
Library of Congress Control Number: 2015908730

Edited by Louise Cook and David J. Sebesta
Cover illustration by Alex McVey
Cover layout by Zach McCain

More from KT Ashely
www.authorktashely.com

For all the kids at the pool—on both sides of the fence.

The Pool

I had heard the word "colored" or some variation thereof most all my young life. But it was not until one particular day in front of the most fascinating machine I had ever known, that I gave it much thought.

The Methodist church fellowship hall somewhere near Houston had a sight to behold. It was a Coke machine like no other. When my father would open it to refill the contents, a world of frigid, metal gears mesmerized me. My imagination went wild. There was a huge spiral in the middle. To me, it looked like the Milky Way galaxy in school science books. The bottles would load into the circling, gray trays. Once the big red door was closed the magic could happen.

To get a Coca-Cola, all you had to do was get a nickel from your mama, put it in the slot, and turn the crank. The gears would churn and clink with great fanfare to the delight of small imaginative children. Then the small, filled glass bottle of treat would pop out with a clatter. However, even with all of that excitement, I was not prepared for what happened next on this peculiar day.

I had not heard all of the conversation. But I had heard enough to spark my interest. A tall man with a neat flat-top, pressed short-sleeved shirt, and black-rim glasses seemed to be making my mom a bit uneasy with the conversation.

"Your husband's people are like the color'ds. In their part of the world."

"My husband is Czech," she said informatively to the man.

"Yeah, I know. That's what I'm sayin'. He's Slavic."

The most I can remember about the conversation was that it was short, it had upset my mother, and I wanted to know more about being "colored". I knew I was Czech. Grandma and Grandpa were. They lived in a Czech community in Burleson County, Texas. Everyone there speaks the Czech language. Their Moravian Brethren Church holds services in Czech. Some there also speak German. To me it all sounded the same. I couldn't understand a word of it. But I thought *colored?*

"Mama", I asked, "what is colored?"

"Well, that's like Mr. Marshall and them at Grandpa's," she replied.

Mr. Marshall helped my Grandpa on the farm. Sometimes when we would go there, Mr. and Mrs. Marshall and their two boys would be there helping bring in the crops. At times a bunch of people would be in the fields picking field peas, corn or baling hay—including my family and my cousins. When we finished for the day, we would all have some watermelon or kolaches or some other treat. All the kids would play while the grown folks did business and talked before heading home.

The Marshall family and others that came to help looked like us. They had arms and legs, and blue shirts and yellow straw hats, and there were boys and girls. The only difference I can recall was that some of their family had different skin tones. Some skin was the color of dark coffee and some skin was the color of rust, like that on the old mule-farm implements.

Other folks had eyes that were brown or blue. Hair was curly, straight, blonde and black. But as far as I knew, everyone there had one thing in common. We were all Czech. Some lived here, some lived there, but we all came to the farm to work the fields at harvest time.

I noticed major changes in my world a few years later. My father was called to be pastor in a place further from the city. We said goodbye to the church with the fantastic Coke machine and to the man who made my mother fearful. Our new town was smaller and we lived close enough to everything so that we could walk and ride our bikes everywhere.

I was older too. The immature preconceived images of *colored people* being more or less vivid, rainbow spectrums, as I had imagined in my earliest of youth, now were waning as well. It was 1969 when we moved, and I was in the later part of elementary school. That is when things started to flux.

We had been living in our new East Texas home for a year or two. The people were different. They were more country. And there were more who had dark skin tones like the Marshall family at the farm. I don't recall any of my Houston teachers looking like that. They all looked like the people at my father's city church—and my Gran. But here I had teachers of all shapes, sizes and colors. And I went to school with children of more diverse skin shades as well.

I liked it here. In fifth grade, I thought I might even join my new friends who called themselves the Black Panthers. They were pretty cool kids with their dark black eye shades and ebony leather coats. We all hung out together and played a game we called *revolution*. We'd always *stick it to the man*. I never really knew who *the man* was, but I was sure he was a very bad individual.

Seasons passed and my body began to change, as did my mind. It was the last two weeks of school in 1971. The summer was coming. Memorial Day was almost here. We would be in the seventh grade next year. Miss Arthur *would be happy to see us off*, she often audibly surmised.

The poor woman must have been fifty if not eighty. She had skin so dark it shined. And despite eating those Ayds diet candies all day, she hadn't lost a single pound that we could tell. Sometimes she would even fall asleep right in the middle of class. That's when Rabbit and some of the other boys would shoot paper spit wads into her hair. Though I couldn't exactly tell if it was a wig or not, her hair was pretty curly and not always tidy. The spit wads stuck smartly in that mess regardless. Rabbit, despite his buckteeth, was an expert marksman with a Bic pen blow pipe. Most of us boys were at that age.

We all seemed to be getting meaner and more talkative, too. Plus, something was starting to happen in our britches. So much so that we would have to keep our hands in our laps at times and refuse to go to the chalk board when called on.

Only Lincoln seemed to be the less aggressive of the bunch. He was my best partner in marbles. When we teamed up on the playground, no one could beat us. He may have been soft spoken, but he dominated in the art of flicking boulders.

It happened on one of the last days of school as we were coming back from lunchroom recess. Bertha Carey and Rickie Strange were best friends. Bertha was Rabbit's sister. He had been held back for two years—most probably for meanness. Regardless, we were all students in Miss Arthur's class.

The classroom had a tall wooden partition built in front of some old metal lockers. The teacher's desk was on the opposite side facing the students. I was putting my sack of marbles into my locker and getting out my social studies book for the up coming lesson, when Bertha and Rickie cornered me behind the wall.

Bertha had beautiful cinnamon skin. She was skinny and her natural hair was usually unkempt and bushed out. Although she often begged Rabbit to let her use his cake-cutter to comb it out, he refused. It seemed she always wore a dirty white T-shirt, some ratty pants, and not much of anything you could call shoes. Her brother dressed the same.

Rickie on the other hand, always appeared scrubbed hard and clean. She was the color of Miss Arthur and always wore a simple, but neatly pressed pinafore dress with a white blouse. Her hair was straight and thick. Her mama always had it in three, large twist-braids. The elastics had big, white plastic balls on the ends. It reminded me of three fancy pony's tails coming off of her head. It was the same head that had a crazy eye and big white teeth that completed the foresaid equine juxtaposition.

"Hey Tony!" Rickie shouted at me. I could smell her old baloney breath as they cornered me against my locker. That crazy eye was fixed on who knows what. Bertha was on the other side of me giggling mischievously.

"What ch'all want?" I asked indignantly.

"Bertha wants ta' show ya' sumthin'!"

As I turned to see what Bertha was up to, she pulled up her dirty white t-shirt and I got the surprise of my life.

There before me, the girl with the beautifully toned skin—much the shade of my own, cackled profusely. My eyes grew wide as I stood in shock gawking at two swollen nee-nee buds of which I had never seen on a girl. Her perfect brown nipples looked nothing like my much younger baby sister's. These were puffy and protruding from her chest ever so slightly. For some reason they made me feel very scared, but enticed at the same time.

I must have let out an audible gasp or squeal because the girls guffawed so loudly, that my returning classmates rushed to see what was happening. Despite the chaos, I managed to retain the grip on my social studies book and claim my seat. As the adrenaline cursed my body, I felt something else twice as embarrassing coming to fruition. It was an erection. I placed my book in my lap to hide my secret. *Cuss those girls* I thought, *just cuss those girls.*

When we had first moved to town years before, we had not gone to the city park's pool much at all. Mama would only take us two or three times a summer. But this was the year of changes. My father had joined the Rotarians. He announced that we could swim more often this summer because he had been appointed as the new pool manager or something like that. All we knew was that in the previous month of April, we had started going there to help him clean the place up.

First we drained out all the dirty water from the season before. Then we raked up all of the muck and old leaves. The inside of the pool well was painted white before it was refilled. We also scrubbed down the bathhouse and the concession stand. Usually my brother and I helped out on Saturdays because Daddy had to preach on Sundays. We still had school during the week.

On the Saturdays that we would go and work, I would see many of my friends from the schoolhouse. They would ride their bikes over, stand at the fence, and watch us work.

The park was usually full of people then. Most were families like those of Rabbit, Lincoln, and their cousins. They had a lot of bar-b-que, music making, and all kinds of fun. I asked Daddy once if we could go sometime and he said that Saturday was the day that the *colored folk* go to the park. I thought, *well alright—since we were colored, and they were Czech too, we outta have a good time.*

But we never went. We just stayed around the pool. Usually, Lincoln and all of us just played marbles outside of the fence in the gravel-dirt parking lot. The best spot was under the oak tree. A mockingbird would always sing loudly there.

Sometimes we would play Army. We would throw green horse apples at each other from a nearby Osage Orange tree. But Daddy always got on to us saying that someone could get hurt. And hurt it did if you got hit by one. That was the point.

The pool opened on Memorial Day weekend with great excitement. My brother aged ten and I eleven, until my birthday in July, were one of the first ones there. At twelve noon on Saturday the front gate was unlocked. Kids ran in screaming. Ryan, the college lifeguard, yelled at them to slow down and take a shower first.

It was to be a promising summer. However, I did notice that some of my friends from school were hanging on the outside of the fence. When I asked my father if they could come in, he told me that every family had to have a membership. I gave that little more thought for the next few weeks.

It became custom for my brother and me to ride our bikes to the pool and swim every single day. The pool was the greatest thing in our lives. As the days passed, our olive skin turned darker and darker. Ryan the lifeguard became one of our best pals. He even let us come into the concession area and sell cold drinks and candy when our father wasn't around. He taught us how to put peanuts in a can of Dr. Pepper to make a special concoction.

Ryan had long wavy and black "pirate hair." His skin was tanned brown. It turned a kind of reddish as the days went on. He said he was part Comanche Indian. When he first told us this, my brother and I were a bit scared. That is because soon after we had first moved to town, a big rather pudgy fellow with a curly flat-top and tight cropped sides of golden hair had visited my father in his church study. Daddy had been unpacking his books.

"Howdy there Pastor. Names Charley Tillis."

"It's a pleasure Charles," my father replied as he seemed to have heard tell of him already.

The two men visited long enough for us to realize that Charley was no man at all. In fact he was just a big old, bull-headed looking junior high school boy who wanted to know about getting a ping pong table for the youth group. Due to his rather humongous size and his wavy topped head with shaved sides, my brother and I decided he looked like one of our Grandpa's polled Herefords. Thus we gave him the nickname "Bull." That name fit our new friend more than we could have currently imagined due to the antics we three would cavort in the years to come.

"Almost got caught by them Injuns," he said as he turned to us and pulled up his western style shirt. The tails were long, his belly big, and the exercise was dramatic as he reeled out the fabric from his tight-waisted jeans. "Got me right there. Had to take to fightin' 'em with my tommie-hawk to get away. Killed two of 'em."

My brother and I were in awe as we stared at a long scar on his right side. It was a flabby side of skin so white that it was almost pink. Bull went on to spin a tale of the horror of almost being "scalped alive" until my father stopped the show. Years later we found out that he had his appendix taken out. How were we supposed to know what that scar was? After all, he was wearing cowboy boots.

Peggy was the female counterpart to our Indian-blooded friend Ryan. They both went to college—she to Southern Methodist University and he to Stephen F. Austin. She was going to be a doctor of something and he was a *thespian*, what ever that was. All we knew was that when Ryan got around Peggy, her blue eyes and long blonde hair made him act and talk like a man in a boring old romance movie at the picture show.

When she came around, he would play Marvin Gaye and the Delfonics on the pool's 8-track stereo. We liked those songs OK, but we preferred to hear Cream and Steppenwolf. He often would crank it up loud when it was mostly just kids swimming. Ryan turned us on to a lot of good music our parents never would have. It certainly was a different sound from their Jim Nabors, Eddie Albert and Johnny Mathis records.

It was a curious thing though—Peggy sitting in her swimsuit on the concession counter. I felt peculiar as I gazed at her there. Her habit was to watch the pool from the breezy sheltered space. She said she liked to sit there and listen to the mockingbirds sing.

The weathered wooden building had one large window on either side and two on the front. They each opened up and inward with a pulley and cotton cord before being secured to the open rafters with a latch hook. The counter was very wide and formed a wrap around "C" shape much like a sitting porch on any old Southern home. The sea green color was touched up every year but past patron's, carved, initials always peeked through the heavy coats of paint.

Peggy would sit there, legs bent up with feet flat. Her arms rested forward on top of her knees as she habitually twirled a long black lanyard that had a silver whistle attached. She stared forward piously surveying from large sepia toned Foster Grant sunglasses which veiled her eyes. Her back rested against the window posts.

When I stood at the counter my head was at her waist. But my eyes were often fixated on her bikini bottom. Early on I was beginning to realize why Ryan was attracted to her. I did not quite understand it, but the curves of her body started to call to me as my ogle ascended. My older friend called them boobs. They were rounding, shapely and about the size of Rio Grande Valley grapefruits. Each hung smartly in a pretty fabric top of which she would change the style daily.

Once, I was climbing on the counter to sit with her. I had retrieved her book as requested. It was then that I espied a similar sight that I had seen only a couple of weeks earlier. However, this time it was curiously different; and I did not flinch.

I hoisted myself up from behind her. A window brace assisted my ascension. There I glimpsed a pink puffy nipple among a most perfect white bosom within her loosely open top. It was somewhat like Bertha's nee-nees, but larger and more formed in shape. I had wondered what it looked like under that top. Her tan lines always peeked out shyly but I never expected to see that. No wonder Ryan was always hanging around.

I was confused but excited at what I saw. Apparently my male lifeguard friend understood much more than I. But my fate was relegated to the younger girls. And for what ever reason, they seemed to become an increasingly enchanting amusement for me. Little did I know that her breasts would not be the only thing I would become enlightened about this summer.

Cindy Heard and Cammie Scott had been friends ever since I had known them. They were in the next grade above me. I never really noticed them much in school but when they started coming to the pool, they received more attention than usual—and not just from me.

Cindy got most of the attention. This may have been because she had now turned thirteen and her mama let her wear a bikini. It had a heart cut-out on the hip. All the boys knew that the design's pattern would allow it to tan through and leave a heart shape there. But no matter how many times we pleaded, she would never show any of us what it looked like on her underlying white skin.

Cammie got a bikini too. The girl gossip was that she only got one because of her incessant begging to her mama, and on account of her best friend's good fortune. The problem had been that Cammie would not make it past twelve until the end of June. Her parents rule was that she had to turn thirteen first. But hers did not sport a cutout like Cindy's.

Never-the-less the girls were a sight. Not because of Cindy's developing curves akin to what Peggy had already achieved, and not because Cammie looked like a toothpick in a two piece—but because of their peculiar habit with lemons.

According to Cammie's high school aged sister, lemon juice bleached hair was the fashion of day. It was all the rage. Both girls had naturally dark hair. Cammie's was chestnut brown and Cindy's was jet black. It being the first week of June we all wondered just exactly what this would look like by the end of their proposed summer ritual.

Not only did that fad take hold, but they and some of the other girls would slather baby oil all over their bodies. They lay in the sun and sizzled. The boys rather liked this routine because what ever was happening to us hormonally also had an affect on our sense of smell. The fragrance of baby oil had never been so revered by us males. Had we been moths, incineration on the front porch light of girl flesh would have been inevitable. Call me Icarus. We were often slapped for attempting to "help" apply the alluring elixir.

The two girls soon became a parody known as the Lemon Sisters. It was not known if they could sing a lick but with all of the beauty enhancement going on we started to observe another curious tick. Greater numbers of lemons began to appear beside them. They weren't just putting the juice in their hair, they were eating the fruit. Cammie was the worst offender. Peggy would say, *I swear that girl eats a dozen lemons every day if not two.*

The girls' hair turned lighter and the days grew longer. With the exception of Bull

Tillis, who just kept getting pinker, most all of us had skin *as dark as Negroes*, the old gray-headed Methodist church ladies would say. And my school friends who had hung on the fence watching us clean the pool in spring, now watched us swim from their side of the fence in summer.

It was a joyful time for us. Families brought their children. Babies splashed in the wading pool while mamas sat as sentries dangling their pale legs in the cool water. The old oak tree in the parking lot reached its limbs over the fence and gave a benevolent shifting shade in that area. It was the domain of the mockingbird. It was a place of respite, innocence and sweet sounds.

Across a grassy verdure lay the big pool. It was the older kid's realm. Boisterous voices echoed throughout the perimeter of the compound.

On the shallow end those just learning their craft swam mostly unmolested. As the waters deepened, the current began to churn. Here games of chase and Marco Polo were played. The splashing increased as if the babies had grown larger and more animated. Bodies torpedoed across and from every side in a congestion of half nakedness and bright colored fabrics. But it was beyond the float rope that the action was at full throttle.

The deep end was only to be explored by the swim masters. Here the offerings included an abyss of twelve ear crushing feet straight down. Two bottom grates could be seen clearly only when the waves had settled calmly. It was rumored that an unfortunate young soul had once been sucked into the single square foot void by foolishly removing one of the protective grills. Presumably, sharks had eaten him once the vortex had spit him out into the open ocean. Only the very brave would venture to dive down deep enough to reach out with nimble fingers and tap the top brass bars before franticly paddling to the surface, never looking back, conserving air, and grasping the safety of the top brick poolside at the surface. No one dared open the grates again nor look too earnestly within—fearing the previous taste of blood would unleash the leviathans beneath the barricade at the bottom of the pool.

There were also diving boards; one high dive and one low dive that were arranged next to each other. As with the ghastly grates, only the most valiant would attempt to climb to the top of the most perilous plank. I had first conquered it at the end of the last summer. But earlier this season, I had to summon courage once more to ascend its steep grade. It was worth it. I could see for streets on end. A good portion of the park, some of the football field in the high school stadium, and something I had not noticed before decorated the lofty vista. It was a fantastic view of the grassy area where all the girls laid out.

My brother and I had surmounted the low dive a few years before. We had mastered the art of flawless cannonballs, preacher's seats, and butt busters from there. In fact, the most exciting thing about the low dive now was when a high school girl named Cynthia Roe would perform a butt buster on it. A butt buster is when you walk to the edge of the board, kick your legs out from under you and bust your bottom on the board causing the daredevil to bounce up—before diving into the water from a seated position. When Cynthia did that, her round bottom jiggled and her busty boobs bounced. All the boys jostled feverishly to get into the board line when she was there.

Despite all the fun we had, one thing kept perplexing me. *Why didn't Lincoln and his little brother Ray Ray ever come in and swim?* I approached the fence. Lincoln had his fingers interlaced between the links. The barrier prevented us from doing a soul shake as we normally did upon greeting each other. We settled for a make shift fist bump that scratched our knuckles on the old galvanized steel between us. "Solid," we said in unison.

"Hey Lincoln, are y'all gonna get a membership so you can swim?"

"Naw. I don't think so. My folks don't have that kinda money" he replied stoically.

"Oh," I said. "Well maybe I can get a pass for y'all from my dad sometime."

"That's cool." Lincoln gazed around me into the pool area when he spoke. He didn't seem to be very interested. The pitch in his voice stayed the same.

After we talked a few more minutes he said, "T'marra is Juneteenth. We're gonna be in the park bar-b-q'in. Y'all wanna come and eat with me and my family?"

"Yeah, I guess so. Wa's june teeth?" I asked.

"Oh it's Freedom Day. Kinda like the Fourth of July." Lincoln looked at me and smiled.

So we agreed that we would meet right here at noontime—but on the other side of the fence. And the next day we did.

My brother and I rode our bikes to the pool through the park just as we did every day. It seemed like any other Saturday. Thick oak and hickory smokes filled the air. Loud music from cars blasted the Jackson 5, and people were gathering all about. In fact, many more people than usual were gathering.

Horse shoes clinked against steel posts set in sand pits and ponies hooves clopped on the black top road. It looked like a parade was about to start. The pool was opening soon, but not many people were lining up to get in. That was odd. We just waited for Lincoln under the oak tree in the parking lot where we had played marbles in the spring.

It was not long before my friend showed up with little Ray Ray riding on the back of his bike. After we exchanged greetings, we rode off to the festivities. My little brother had come along with me, too.

I was surprised to see so many people that I knew from school. All of their families were there. Miss Florentine, who we called Miss Flo, was one of the first to greet us. She was my mama and daddy's best friend's maid. Miss Flo babysat the McConnell girls at their house. Mr. McConnell was a lawyer in town. I heard him and my daddy talking one time about how they *marry 'em and bury 'em* and that they should just go into business together. I didn't much know what that meant, but Mama said something about them doing weddings and wills. That just confused me even more so I stopped asking about it.

Miss Flo was always good to us when we visited. She made the best molasses cookies anyone had ever tasted. I was hoping that she had brought some. It turns out she had; Miss Arthur showed up with the plateful and offered us one under the direction of our newly, self-appointed chaperon. I had no idea that Miss Arthur was Miss Flo's cousin. It was then that I began to wonder just what the two ladies had shared about me over the previous year. At least my name wasn't *Rabbit* I decided. The anxious thoughts soon left my imagination.

After many reunions with school friends, a quick game of *no keepers* marbles, and an encounter with my nemeses Bertha

Carey and Rickie Strange, we sat down to eat. The park's table furnishings were long concrete slabs with benches made of the same material. The tops had been covered with colorful cloth that reminded me of my grandmother's quilts. All types of food had been placed before us. But before we could touch anything, an old dark-skinned and white-haired gentleman they called Preacher spoke.

And spoke he did. He delivered a prayer so long that he even out prayed my daddy in church. I never knew anyone to have that much wind—not even a Baptist. But the gentle and pitching cadence of his words amazed me. Lincoln not so much; he was sitting on the one side of me and my brother was on the other side. My friend kept fidgeting about. I and my sibling knew better than to make a move so close to the grown folks. Lincoln eventually got a stern *shush* from Miss Florentine who was being piously attentive just across the table from us. He was lucky enough not to get a slap or even worse, *a switchin'*.

I do remember one part of the invocation though. It was curious to me because although it sounded curiously familiar to what we had learned in school, it also was different in some way. Mr. Preacher pulled out a paper from his coat pocket, and said this before praying over the food:

"On this day here, June nineteenth in 1865, the Union Major General Gordon Granger read the General Orders Number 3 to the people of Galveston. It so did state,"

The people of Texas are informed that, in accordance with a proclamation from the Executive of the United States, all slaves are free. This involves an absolute equality of personal rights and rights of property between former masters and slaves, and the connection heretofore existing between them becomes that between employer and hired labor. The freedmen are advised to remain quietly at their present homes and work for wages. They are informed that they will not be allowed to collect at military posts and that they will not be supported in idleness either there or elsewhere.

"Thank you sweet Jesus," he added and then continued the blessing with bowed head.

The wait to eat was worth it. Folks started passing greens, hominy, pinto beans, corn on the cob, hot water corn bread, and some of the biggest biscuits I'd ever seen. They were accompanied with Mayhaw jelly, cane syrup and farm fresh butter just like at my grandma's.

There were pickles of every kind. Among them were bread and butters, dills, pickled beets and my all time favorite— spiced and pickled Indian peaches. We had Big Red cold drink, ice tea and fresh squeezed lemonade that someone had made.

When the meats came off the pit, it reminded us of the German barbeque in Deanville we would get on the Fourth of July. Every year when we went to the farm for the holiday, Grandpa and all the boy cousins and uncles would go the Sons of Hermann grounds and dance hall. It was a fraternal order like our own Czech SPJST.

We visited different pits specializing in various meat choices of beef, pork or mutton. The air was always thick with the aroma of smoky meats and mixed dialects. We felt right at home here, too. The many tongues spoken were much the same to my ears.

The people were similar to Grandma's and Grandpa's as well. Some looked like the Marshall family. Others had lighter skin and still others even darker. Two twin girls stood out from the rest of the group though. They wore thick glasses and had very pale blue eyes with skin as white as a sheet. Their hair was like Bertha Carey's, only it was towheaded and combed neatly into an afro. Curiously, their mama and daddy had a more cinnamon toned skin like Bertha's.

Lincoln said they were kinfolks from Louisiana. Their daddy was the one who had brought the sausage they called *boudin*. They spoke like no one I had ever heard before. Lincoln said it was called Cajun French. He said his Uncle Red spoke some of that language and that it helped him out when he was in a place called Nam.

Uncle Red had black straight hair like mine and my brothers. I heard a couple of ladies commenting on it. They called it *good hair*. It was long and a bit like Ryan's but not as wavy. His skin looked a little red but more like a handsome rust color to me. Lincoln told us he had Indian blood in him, that's why people called him Red. The twin's daddy just called him 'ol Redbone. They acted like they were pretty good friends.

Someone said that Lincoln's uncle had been in *the war* fighting yellow people in a jungle. Uncle Red called them gooks. I could understand *red* people like Indians, but they weren't really red like a stop sign. I knew something about *the war* because my mama said her brother Uncle Ben had been there. Sometimes we saw pictures they called *the war* on TV when Mr. Cronkite would come on, but my mama always made us leave the room when that show started. My daddy used to watch Mr. Cronkite every night. But I couldn't grasp the concept of yellow people. I didn't know anyone like that and all the people on the TV just looked as if they were many different shades of gray.

Everyone was having a really good time eating, visiting, and listening to the music playing. Some folks were singing songs and hymns in the background. I knew some of them. It was kind of like being in church outside.

As we were starting to make plans for dessert, Rabbit's older brother and some of his friends came up and said to the group,

"Why y'all mixin' wit-dese white chu'rens? Dey ain't no black folk."

My brother and I looked over at the pale skinned twins. But while the young man who was dressed like a Black Panther stood over us—we realized he was looking down at the two of *us* through his dark lens glasses.

It was then that Miss Florentine stood up from across the table and said, "Take yo' rag'aty ass on outta he'ah, nigger."

My brother and I knew that word. It was a cuss word. And we were surprised to hear it from Miss Flo. She hadn't said *nigga* like I had been hearing from time to time during the day—a word my friends would say to each other on the play ground at school. And she hadn't said Negro.

Being around the word *nigga* so much at school, my brother and I had incorporated it into common place *trash talk* directed at each other. My friends Lincoln and Rabbit said it all the time when we popped marbles. But we never, ever would say what she had just said. Our daddy would have whooped us senseless with the belt. Even though *nigga* was lower down on the severity of whoopins scale, if our mama heard us say it she would slap us silly and tell us not to talk like that.

And we never talked trash around Daddy. It was shocking to hear Miss Florentine cuss like that. All afternoon when someone around her did say *nigga*, she would scold them and say to stop all that trash talking. But no sir, it was clear she had used the big cuss word.

This other word was different. It changed the mood at the table. Or at least we thought the silence was because of her cussing. In any event, two men and Uncle Red stood up without saying anything. I thought they were going to have words with Miss Flo, but they just glared at Rabbit's brother and his friends. The unwelcome visitors moved on without another utterance. After a confusing few moments of silence, someone asked us if we wanted some more to eat, and the mood gradually became festive again.

It wasn't long before the table had been cleared and desserts started to appear. Many folks had scattered and were sitting in lawn chairs or on stumps or blankets visiting with kin. Uncle Red made a space on the empty corner of the bench so we could take turns cranking the ice cream bucket. Ray Ray was sitting on his grandmother's lap whom they called Big Mama. He was helping her to slice up strawberries. Getting to turn the crank was almost as fun as eating the fresh strawberry ice cream.

The twin's daddy had a machine, too. He was using fresh peaches. It was so curious about the twins. Their mama, daddy and baby brother had cinnamon skin. I just couldn't understand why the girls were so pale looking like the ice cream. They were even whiter than Bull Tillis. It would be a pondered thought for years to come. Albinism was not yet a word in my vocabulary.

The table had been reset with a various selection of sweets and fruits. Pies ranged from pecan to lemon meringue to dewberry cobbler. There was red velvet, chocolate, 7UP, and oatmeal cake. Each looked like they should win the blue ribbon at the county fair and livestock show. But when the Black Diamond watermelons were pulled from the ice water and Big Mama skillfully cracked them open on the table, I wasn't sure if I wanted the melon or the ice cream first. There were both kinds of diamond melons— ruby red meat and golden yellow meat. Each one was as sweet as the other. But still, the initial decision had to be made.

It was a fine day. We felt excited about the whole thing because we knew a similar event would be repeated in a couple of more weeks at my grandparent's house. We would see most of our cousins on the Fourth. But for now, we were content with knowing that we had family right here in our own little town. It was family that loved, protected, and accepted us.

The long afternoon was coming to a close. What little leftover food there was had been packed up. The big pile of watermelon rinds from everyone's leavings were put in bread bags and made ready for a pickling party at Big Mama's house. Miss Flo gave us a hug and told us to remember her to our folks. We thanked Lincoln for inviting us and told him what a good time we had. We gave a final goodbye to our friends, old and new before hopping onto our bikes to swim in the remaining few minutes that the pool would be open.

But for me, it would not be without first dodging a gauntlet of Bertha Carey and Rickie Strange. They pawed at me and almost knocked me off my bike as I tried to get away from their affections. Lincoln helped to block old crazy eye, but Bertha managed to grab me by the shirt before I was able to tug loose. Her pursed lips were only inches from mine. *Cuss those girls* I thought, *just cuss those girls*. My brother just laughed and started making kissing sounds at me with his mouth. *Cuss him too.*

———————

Every summer we looked forward to seeing our cousins at the farm. Daddy didn't have to preach for a week, so that meant we didn't have to go to church or Sunday school either. Not only did we get a reprieve from being bored to death in the sanctuary, but we also caught a break from Miss Cappadocia Crell—the meanest Sunday school teacher that ever lived. She hoarded gold stars like a dragon hoards treasure. Even her name was atrocious. Perhaps it was just us, but it seemed that everyone else got a glimmering celestial prize for reciting bible verses every week. My brother and I just got a stern…*try again*.

It was our ill fated luck that this summer's plans had been superseded. We got to go to the farm alright but only for two days. The rest of the time we had to visit our Gran in Austin. That was even more boring than church. Our parent's compromising promise made during travel for *a good time at Gran's*, was to be highlighted by a fireworks show and a trip to Barton Springs—the most fantastic of all pools. All was negotiated under duress.

My mom's mom was a retired schoolmarm. She hated kids like my brother and me. The feeling was mutual. Every time we wanted to play with our Hot Wheels cars, she scolded us about the time we allegedly marked up her coffee table. We now had to play with them on her white shag carpet. Every boy knows that cars will not roll on shag carpet.

There also was a wooden box on that table that had something secret inside. If we even looked at it sideways my Gran would give us the stink eye. Mama constantly kept up a vigil watching to make sure we didn't open that little brown box. To make it worse, one time when we did get the chance to sneak a look inside, it was locked. That box became even more of a nemesis than Bertha Carey.

We had to *just sit and be quiet* on the sofa most of the time that we were there. It was a hard sofa. I imagined cavemen had softer rocks to recline on. My Gran had the oddest painting hanging over it. It was a picture called *The Three Musicians* by *Pistachio* or somebody. I never understood what that was all about. The only thing that made any sense to me about that painting was that some guy with a beard was in it. But it was always there—a creepy reminder of my penitence in this place for scratching up a dumb old table.

Austin was a large place. Its breadth reminded me of Houston a little bit from what I could remember. It wasn't a dusty city like our little town that was dotted with cotton gins on the edge of town. This was a clean place.

The neighborhood my grandmother lived in looked like it had been scrubbed clean. It was a well groomed affluent looking space with lush green grass. Although the houses were close together, the yards were plush and shady.

All the homes in her neighborhood looked new. My Gran's house, as well as others, was built with white river rock. The smooth stones felt cold to the touch. They always smelled like fresh rain. There was a tall Sycamore tree in her front yard. Unlucky for us, it had a bark that was excruciatingly tempting to peel.

The dirt in the flower beds around the house was a rich licorice black. Again, to our demise, we enjoyed the way it felt in our hands. Mexican blackbirds cackled incessantly throughout the day from tree to tree. My brother and I had not one BB between us. Red Ryder could have put a stop to that.

As soon as we parked on the street in front of her house, we could see her white Dodge Dart in the driveway. That car was even more *old ladyish* than the Ford station wagon that had brought us here. There was no miraculous hope that she had somehow forgotten we were coming and that we could high tail it back to the farm to play with my cousins.

The arrival was uneventful. No honking the horn on the way up the red-rock pasture road, or as we went across the cow-guard. No dogs barking and chasing the car. No smiling grandma standing on the porch wiping the flour from her soft hands onto her apron. No scent of fresh baked kolaches wafting in the country air. No, this was purgatory, and I knew exactly what was behind that forlorn, dark door we were about to pass through.

"Hey, Mama!" my mother exclaimed.

"Oh Honey, how are you…son. Y'all come on in. Have a seat," the receiving woman greeted.

Yeah…on that Stone Age couch I thought. She looked right at my brother and me as we reluctantly brought up the rear of the unpardoned parade.

"Don't touch anything on that table," she hissed from behind a pair of rhinestone, black cat-eye glasses. Her wrinkled and old crooked finger poked at us like a knotty stick. It was the same finger that Cappadocia Crell would point at us. Those fingers could have only been forged in one place. The bad place that rhymed with what my brother and I often called Miss Crell behind her back. And the devil knew it to be true.

"Well, look at you boys," a deep gruff voice said as we entered the living room.

"Uncle Ben!" we shouted.

Our Uncle Ben was our favorite uncle. It was rare that we got to see him, but when we did he always made it a good time. He lived in San Antonio. My mama said he worked for the government. He was a spy or something for the Army. His briefcase was black, but I never saw it handcuffed to his wrist. He had been in the war like Lincoln's Uncle Red. I never thought to ask if they knew each other.

"What cha' eatin', Uncle Ben?" I asked.

"Oysters."

I gave him a curious glance. He was sitting at my Gran's breakfast bar with a plate of grey things in shells that looked like they were swimming in a pool of liquid. Beside him were lemon wedges, some horseradish, ketchup, and Tabasco red pepper sauce in a little bottle.

"Wanna try one?" he asked.

I wasn't completely sure I did. They looked kind of old and wet. Frankly they looked like a big grey loogie.

"Skert?" my brother taunted, but I had seen his face, too. I knew he had no intention of eating one. But I wasn't going to be bested by my brother.

"OK," I blurted. The words came out of my mouth just as quickly as if my knee had been thumped at the doctor's office. *Cuss my brother.* I was committed now.

Uncle Ben methodically organized the event as if he had been presenting to the King of England. Apparently there was certain protocol to preparing the prize.

"OK," he said as he stabbed the soft flesh with a tiny fork. "First you squeeze a little lemon. Then you dab a bit of ketchup. I'm gonna leave off the Tabasco sauce. Then a spot of horseradish."

I didn't much care that he left off the pepper sauce. A previous experience with that stuff left me thankful I would not be trying it again. But I did wonder aloud to him, "What's that stuff it's sittin' in?"

"Oh, that's the best part of all," my Uncle replied. "It's the tears of the Walrus."

I knew what a walrus was. We had studied them in science class. But looking at those oysters, thinking about the tears and associating the two with crying and something that was beginning to closely resemble what my grandpa called mountain oysters, filling a bucket up at the springtime pig castration—I was beginning to have doubts about what I was doing there.

"Now just give a slurp into your mouth as I hold the shell for ya'. Don't chew much, just kinda swallow it."

I did as I was told. The salty brine of the tears was the first pleasant sensation; next followed the tasty familiar flavor of cocktail sauce. As this was going on, my Uncle began to recite something familiar to my ears, but my concentration was aloof.

"I weep for you," the Walrus said:
"I deeply sympathize."
With sobs and tears he sorted out
Those of the largest size,
Holding his pocket-handkerchief
Before his streaming eyes.

As Uncle Ben began to express the words *Holding his pocket-handkerchief*, I began to chew. And chew. And I chewed I fear too long because the thing in my mouth began to grow. And grow it did to a point that I was in conflicting consideration as to either swallow or spit. With my bother giggling on one side and my Uncle encouraging me from the other, I forced down the offending parcel. It slid down just like the loogie I had first imagined but had the girth of a rock that I feared would lodge in my constricting throat.

"Well hey, how was that?"

"Great," I croaked out.

"You're a real man now," my Uncle congratulated as he patted my back and unwittingly helped the oyster to slime down.

"Yeah, I'll try it again sometime," I replied before walking away. *But not in this lifetime* was my thought.

He promptly went back to his ritual of dressing the poor fellows and slurping each one, but not before reciting another verse of poetry from The Walrus and the Carpenter.

> *"But wait a bit," the Oysters cried,*
> *"Before we have our chat;*
> *For some of us are out of breath,*
> *And all of us are fat!"*
> *"No hurry!" said the Carpenter.*
> *They thanked him much for that.*

My Gran just looked at me with a wicked grin as I made my way to the sofa with the curious painting above it. *Lord knows what this trip was going to be like.*

The next day was an unexpected pleasure. We got to go to the pool. Barton Springs Pool was a man made section of Barton Creek located in Zilker Park. The spring fed basin had a sandy creek bottom outlined with limestone banks and a large sloping grassy knoll for sunbathing. A dam kept the measured aquamarine water contained before flowing on. We were always amazed at the natural beauty of the place. But on this day, seeing my Gran in her ancient swimming costume brought my brother and me even more astonishment.

The whole clan, including my Uncle Ben, went to swim. But Gran was the standout. She wore a zebra striped, one-piece suit and a white, rubber, swim cap. It was decorated with a floppy daisy. I was sure that she would wear those cat-eye glasses into the water as well. I was soon confirmed correct.

We splashed in the cool water for sometime before I realized that this pool was far different from the one at home. The size was larger. It seemed to be ten times as big. The bottom was sandy and had concrete steps. The water wasn't chlorinated; it was clean and clear like rain. There were limestone banks that I had the guarded urge to climb. All of those things were different, but when I looked up on the grassy bank and saw my uncle—there was the most difference.

Uncle Ben was reclining next to a tan, long-legged girl about his age. She reminded me of Peggy but had brown hair. She also had no top on. This began to excite me. I had been to this pool many times over the years, but never paid any attention to the partially nude girls. It was as natural a scene as anything in this place.

I wasn't sure why I felt this way. But after spying the girl with Uncle Ben, I was hoping I would not have a situation in my swimming trunks. I didn't have a book to hide it with. Thank goodness the water was cold—it seemed to help.

My eyes wandered and I further had the epiphany that all sorts of people were enjoying themselves. Some families looked like those of Lincoln and Ray Ray's. Others were Mexican that looked like children in pictures my Gran had in her home. It seemed as though I was observing the world as being a disparate place, yet so akin.

Mama called us out of the water for lunch. Uncle Ben stayed with his lady friend a few yards away. I couldn't help but continue to notice her while eating my sandwich.

"Well, young man, it seems you have an interest in young ladies," my Gran declared to me. "Remind me not to allow you to look at any of my National Geographics with Watusi in them."

"What?" I asked, surprised that she had caught me. I was also confused about what she had just said to me in a partial language I had never heard.

"The Watusi. They are a tribe in Africa whose women's breasts are naked."

Holy crap! Not that she had called me out, but that she had called me out in ear shot of Mama.

"Mama! Oh Mama, look who it is!" my mother exclaimed as she hurried away from us.

I was saved from certain humiliation at the hands of my Gran when my mother got up to greet some apparent friends coming our way.

"Buenas tardes Maestra," a handsome and tall, dark skinned man greeted my Gran. She embraced him as if he were her son.

"Jesus," she cheerfully sighed.

The greetings lasted several minutes. Even my Uncle Ben was lured away from his naked counterpart. My mother was speaking with a woman about her age with two boys that mirrored my brother and me.

It turned out that Jesus and Gloria had been my Gran's students when she taught at Southside Elementary school in San Marcos. It was the school that the Mexican children attended. She also had been the Visiting Teacher; a teacher that would go to the home of the homebound children to teach. Uncle Ben and my mother would sometimes go to Gloria's house with my Gran to teach her infirmed sister. My mother and Gloria became friends as did my uncle and Jesus— who was Gloria's brother's playmate. Despite the group attending separate schools, they became lifetime amigos. Gloria and Jesus later married.

We continued to enjoy a grand lunch. Everyone shared some of what they had brought. Gran was a huge fan of French food. She had often traveled to Paris in the 1920's as did most her affluent counterparts of the era. She made us chicken salad sandwiches with fresh herbs. Miss Gloria brought the best tamales and lengua tortas that I have ever tasted to this day. She also brought horchata. My Gran had made fresh raspberry mint lemonade from herbs in her backyard garden.

The adults reminisced about the old days while we waited for lunch to settle before we could swim again. I found out that my Gran had been in a boarding school. Her best friend's father was a prominent movie producer in Mexico City. One summer she was invited for a visit. While there, the two girls were chosen as extras to be in one of his movies.

Years later, my Gran got a letter from her friend. She told her that they were re-releasing some of the old features that her father had produced. The film they were in was to be played at the Hayes Theater in San Marcos. It was the Spanish speaking show that accommodated the large Latino population there. Gran took Mama and Uncle Ben to see the movie that she was in.

My father also had a story from the area that he shared with us. While at

Southwest Texas State Teacher's College, *the school that President LBJ had graduated from*—of which he emphasized smartly, my father had taught junior high Sunday school. The class was at Iglesia Presbiteriana. He said he taught in English but that the church services were held in Spanish. Daddy added that he had kept his hymnal from there and agreed to bring it to Grandmas sometime so we could sing hymns from it.

We always had singing time at the farm, despite the dog's obvious disagreement. They would howl loudly from the porch as my grandmother played her pump organ. We sang louder still. I could only imagine what they might do when we all tried to sing in Spanish.

As the day grew longer, we swam and played with our new found friends. All were there splashing and enjoying each other's company. Every color of child was there, much like the rainbow people I had imagined in my earliest youth. None of us children knew that society had given us names other than what our families had called us. Anything else was what grown folks said. We all just enjoyed the day in the aquamarine pool. The prism of each splash in sunlight echoed the color of our own bodies.

Later that evening, before the fireworks started, someone on a loud speaker led the crowd in the Pledge of Allegiance. In a way, it reminded me of the prayer that Mr. Preacher had said at Juneteenth. Then a fabulous burst of color exploded over our heads. All of us lay side by side in family groups on blankets throughout the park, celebrating our nation's Independence Day. I wished Lincoln could have come; not just for the fireworks, but to have swum.

Mama helped Gran fix breakfast the next morning. She was big on grapefruit. I thought that fruit was about as sour as she was. But curiously, today it seemed a little sweeter. Perhaps my attitude about being stuck there was emendable. It would not be too much longer before I realized just how much.

"I didn't know y'all spoke Spanish," I said as my brother slurped up his breakfast citrus. A special spoon clinked when he hit the sides of his bowl with it. We liked those spoons. They had a funky sawtooth on the sides to dig the flesh out with.

"There's a lot you don't know, son," my Gran said directly.

"Well, I know I don't know what a Watusi is."

She looked at me cross-eyed from those hideous glasses. But it wasn't the stink eye. And then she really surprised me.

"When we finish breakfast and you wash your hands clean and dry, I will show you."

"OK," I said. Like the *OK* I had confirmed to Uncle Ben at the start of oyster eating odyssey. I was hoping it would not be any worse. This was Gran after all.

The kitchen was cleared of breakfast dishes from the bar. My sister began to irritate my brother about playing with his Hot Wheels cars. Both my parents hustled about to get ready for a trip to the grocery. I just sat clean and dry on the Neanderthal instrument-of-torture and waited quietly. Pistachio's crew looked down on me from above. The little wooden box on the coffee table was begging me to touch it. I resisted, reluctantly.

"Aright, let's go everybody," Daddy called.

Gran stood in the kitchen with her hand on her hip, drinking herbal tea, and looking straight at me before saying, "Why don't you stay here with me."

I looked at my mother and her at me. She said, "You want to?"

"Yeah," I squeaked out, hoping I wasn't about to meet the fate of Gretel's brother in the Grimm's Fairy Tale book.

I was deep in it now. When my family left, it was only the two of us. I didn't know if Uncle Ben had gone back home to San Antonio or not. All I knew was that he hadn't come with us last night. In fact, the last time I saw him he was with that long legged lady at the pool.

Gran said, "Come here. I want to show you something."

As she gave me the command, my grandmother opened the kitchen's door to her garage. It made an eerie squealing sound. Darkness seemed to creep out from the pitch black inside. *Yeah, this is what Hansel saw before he was pushed into the oven* I thought.

Just before I reached the doorway, Gran flipped on the light. Although the space was small, it had several large bookcases with glass fronts positioned against a far wall. They were filled with books and yellow covered magazines from floor to ceiling. I hadn't remembered ever seeing this room. It was *only* the garage, and in any event Gran was quite particular about where we explored.

The chamber was just as neat and tidy as the interior of her home. But this was no garage. A sitting area had been made. The floor was carpeted and it smelled like the Library. There were statues of both white marble and black bronze; some of which I recognized from my mother's art books she sometimes let us look at. There also was an old photograph of a soldier in a weird, glass frame. It bowed out and the picture looked like it had been painted with watercolors or something.

"This is my collection of National Geographic Magazine," Gran stated. She gave a wave as if she were Moses parting the Red Sea. "I have been collecting them since I was twelve. The first issue I received was from my father in 1912. It was a birthday gift."

I stood before the massive collection, amazed. I had seen these types of magazines before in the library at home, but even they didn't have this many.

Gran went over to a section that looked faded from the rest. The yellow color was much paler. She knew exactly which one she wanted, as if she knew the proper place of each one.

"Have a seat on the settee and turn on the lamp dear."

Dear? When had she ever called me that? But I did as I was told. *What? Did she get all of her furniture from a caveman or something?* The sofa's fabric was garish. Decorative trim outlined it with all kinds of wood work typically found in old lady houses.

Gran retrieved two magazines. She sat down as close as she ever had, next to me, and said, "This French settee was given to me and your grandfather on our wedding day. My parents had it shipped from Paris. It's stuffed with horse hair. It is very good for the posture."

Posture? I'm sitting on a deceased horse? How long has it been dead? No wonder it's as hard as a rock, I thought.

Gazing across the room I asked Gran, "Is that your father in that picture of the soldier?"

"Oh no, dear, that's Benjamin Franklin Bourbon. He's your mother's father. Your grandfather. And he gave me that painting of the horses over there. It's called *The Horse Fair* by *Rosa Bonheur*.

My grandfather? My mother hardly ever spoke about him. I never knew him. "Gran. What happened to him?"

"Oh, dear, he died."

"Well, when? In the war with Uncle Ben or something?" I pressed.

"No son. He was in a war, but not this one. The First World War. He was gassed in the trenches. It caused him to have a terrible lung disease. He lived for several years afterwards. He was a prominent lawyer in San Antonio. Your mother was about five when he died."

"He died from the lung disease?"

"No. Why are you asking so many questions? I wanted to show you this article about the Watusi."

"Mama never talks about him. I just wanted to know."

Gran put the magazines in her lap and folded her hands over them. "Alright. I guess you are getting old enough to know something about the world," she started.

"Your grandfather and I came from affluent families. We traveled all over Europe when we were younger. We would take the ships across the sea. The cabins were beautiful. We loved Paris so much. That is why I have so many lovely reminders from there. His people are originally from France."

"So you're rich?" I inquired bluntly.

Gran gave a humble giggle. "No. At least not anymore. During the 1920's we did have quite a bit of money. But later that decade, the stock market crashed and everyone lost just about everything. That was the start of the Great Depression. Your grandfather and I lived in San Antonio then. Benjamin did the best he could as an attorney, but we had a lot of debt. We had to sell off quite a few things at first."

"But you kept this loveseat?"

She looked at me curiously.

"Yes I did," she confirmed. "Anyway, we loved to dance and listen to music. Don Albert was a musician from New Orleans. We loved New Orleans. It reminded us of France in a way. Mr. Albert opened a nightclub on the eastside of San Antonio. It was in the quarters—the Negro district. Mr. Albert had all sorts of bands come and play.

Many were from the "Chitlin' Circuit." Everyone of all colors came to the place. It was a big deal back then—for people of different races to mix like that. Not like it is today. But then, San Antonio was different from most places in the South."

Chitlins? I knew those. They stunk. But they did taste alright in the greens we had at Juneteenth. I think Miss Flo made them. They were a little chewy. Someone else fried some crispy like those onions Mama puts on green bean casserole. They were good.

She continued, "Well, one night we were walking back to our car and Benjamin and I saw a car full of white segregationists speed up to a mixed couple—a Negro man and a white woman. They jumped out and started beating them. Your grandfather ran over to help the couple and the men started beating him as well. We don't know if it was complications from his afflicted lungs, or if it was just the overexertion that caused the heart attack, but he died soon after being beaten."

I stared at the soldier on the wall. I wished I had known him. Mama never talked about him. Now I knew something at least.

"OK, let's look at these magazines." She changed the subject quickly in a broken voice. Her eyes looked watery. "This is the first one my father gave me. It is from April of 1912."

She carefully turned the pages with her forefinger and said, "Always turn a page from the top outside corner. Gently."

She then placed the priceless artifact in my lap. I knew it was old and dear to her. It made me afraid to touch it. But at the same time, I felt curiously honored that this once perceived mean-old-woman would actually trust me to handle the fragile paper. After all, it wasn't near as indestructible as some old coffee table.

The title of the article was *A Land of Giants and Pygmies*, by some guy named Duke. As soon as I saw the picture, I was excited. It looked just like Mae Annie—a girl in my fifth grade class. The words under the photograph reported it to be *A Watussi in German East Africa*. I was intrigued. *Giants, Pygmies, Germans? WOW! What's goin' on?* I was holding an article with Bible story, comic book, and Tom and Jerry cartoon characters blended together with enemy Germans in the jungle. Gran was *Solid*!

As I carefully turned each page, my grandmother doted over my shoulder with abounding affection. This was a new side of her, I thought. Or was it one that I not always embraced?

We read together and enjoyed a wonderful story about how Mr. Duke had pitched his tent under a tree with a bee hive. All of a sudden the bees attacked everyone and it was a cheerful story indeed.

But as I read on, intrigued with the tall leaping men and a gift of what seemed to be an entire farm, I found a disturbing word.

"Gran," I said as I pointed to the page, "there's a cuss word in here."

My Gran looked at the place where my finger had marked the page. She said matter-of-factly, "Niggers."

I was not sure what to think. *Did Gran just say that? What—is she gonna slap herself for cussin'? 'Cause, I sure the cuss ain't gonna do it.*

"Yes. That is a bad word. Or it is now. Back in those days, the word was used by some to refer to the Negro people. Mostly to American Negroes. Now we do not use that word. In fact, now saying Negro is becoming uncommon. The word we use now is Black. We say Black people. Not the other words."

I knew my Gran had been a teacher for many years. But I had never heard any of my teachers explain anything like this to me. Or enlighten me on so much about the world. In my book, Gran was becoming not just *Solid*, but *Stone Cold Solid*. And *Cool*.

She showed me another National Geographic article—this one was in an issue from December of 1954. It was titled *Safari from Congo to Cairo*. It was similar to the same as before except the pictures were in color. It also had a better picture of the Pygmies. I had learned that there were different tribes of the small people and that they lived mostly in the jungles of various central African countries. I imagined Ray Ray and my little sister as being Pygmies. My sister would have looked just like one of the twins from Louisiana—small and white.

Both Gran and I had agreed that this was our favorite magazine. She said that she had always wanted to go on safari in Africa because of these articles on the Watusi giants and the Wambutti pygmies. But she never did go, she explained, because Mama's daddy had died. She had to use her college degree as a teacher to find a job and support her children. The family never recovered the loss of wealth they had before the Depression.

When it was time to leave our Gran's house for home, I felt sad. It had actually been a good time. I had a different understanding of my grandmother. She had enlightened me on things I had not known or perhaps not noticed. She was willing to share things that my parents would not. I felt as if I had been prepared for something. It felt as if I were flapping my wings like a Mockingbird chick before flying away from the pool. Maybe that is why Peggy always sat on the counter—watching the birds soar over the fence and be free.

Since we had left early, we got home by mid-afternoon. Daddy asked me a few hours later if I wanted to go with him to the pool to run the filters. He thought Ryan had probably been slack on it while we were away, so he wanted to check the chlorine levels before it got dark. This also would give my brother and me a chance to have the closed pool to ourselves. A reprieve from being told that we could not go out earlier.

Just as we pulled into the parking lot, we saw several boys scrambling out of the water. Some ran toward the bath houses and some scaled the fence. My father sighed deeply.

"What's going on, Daddy?" my younger brother asked.

"Just some kids wanting to swim," he replied.

Daddy unlocked the gate. We went into the fenced property. Before my father did anything else, he went to the side of the bathhouse and said loudly, "I know y'all want to swim. There's no lifeguard. I'm afraid someone will get hurt or drown." His face looked concerned, but also sad in some way.

A tall boy that looked familiar, but whom I couldn't place, came out of the men's changing room. He was as tall as my father. He looked like he was a high school kid. After a moment, I recognized him. He was one of the boys that Miss Florentine had cursed at Juneteenth. But this time he didn't have on his black shades or leather jacket. He didn't look like he was so old now. He just looked like any other big kid.

"We jus' wan'da' swim, suh. Ther' ain' no otha' poo."

"I know, son," my father said. The two looked silently at each other for a moment. My brother and I heard nervous feet shuffling in the bathhouse next to us. We looked at each other inquisitively.

Before turning to us, my daddy said "I'll come back tomorrow to finish up."

Somehow we knew we were not going to be able to swim. We just left the grounds. Daddy locked the gate back up and we got into the car.

As we were driving away, I looked back. I was not sure, but it looked like Lincoln and Rabbit were poking their heads out from the entrance of the changing room. A few other dark figures scampered across the back fence in the twilight. A nearly inaudible splash rang through the open window of our white Ford station wagon as we winded through the park. The remainder of the ride home was silent. No one said anything.

———————

"Rock the poooool!" was the rambunctious shout. Bull Tillis had bellowed the call to action. He had taken advantage of the moment as Ryan was tending to a little kid's unfortunate demise of stepping upon a cold drink pull-tab. Just as he was administering a band aid to the child's foot, all Hades broke loose.

Children began running from every direction of the confines to the water. Cannonballs, preacher seats, belly flops, and plain, unabashed mayhem ensued as patrons jumped into the water all at once—nearly missing the fool who had jumped in before him. Ryan scrambled for his whistle. His hands fumbled with the lanyard. But it was too late; no one cared or could have heard him regardless. The pool became a tempest of flailing bodies and buckets of water spewing from the wave action.

Again and again, children would quickly exit and then splash back in. As Cindy Heard was climbing out of the deep end from the ladder, Bull Tillis grabbed her bikini bottom and pulled it down. The glare from her glorious, white, "shiney-hiney," with the obscure heart-shaped, sun tattoo—

seared our eyeballs from its reflection. She backhanded him senseless.

Ryan was livid. He tried to blow his whistle as he ran from the baby pool to his lifeguard chair, but got tripped up in the grass and fell. This only added to the debauchery. He was the only one not laughing and squealing. Red faced and sweaty, he managed to clamor to his knees. The lifeguard spread his arms like Gran, and Moses parting the Red Sea. He then spewed a whistle full of spit with a hearkening blow of minimal pitch.

Exhausted by the affair, Ryan finally dropped his arms in defeat. He hung his head as if he were Jesus in the Garden of Gethsemane. His long dark curly hair dangled. We were not sure if he was praying or crying. Nevertheless, the transgressions naturally receded once everyone tired of the fun. The water level was lowered at least a foot.

Most of the violators returned to their places on sun warmed towels. We all knew what was coming next. Ryan ordered the remaining offenders out of the pool.

As he passed my brother and me he said, "I'm telling your dad." *Like I hadn't heard that before.* After all, we were preacher's kids.

"The pool is closed for thirty minutes!" he addressed the group. "Nobody goes in."

Ryan gave us all the evil eye and then walked back to his "comfy spot" in the shade. It was by the concession counter where Peggy usually sat. But this time, she was not there to give him solace. He was all alone. Her shift had not yet started.

The young patrons of the pool quietly congratulated each other, and planned among themselves another day of shenanigans yet to be announced. Ryan sat in Peggy's spot humiliated. He glanced over at our group only once, just briefly, with sun reddened eyes during the entire punishment.

The next few days were pretty much the same with the exception of an unusual summer rainy spell. My brother and I went to the church with my father one stormy morning, and waited for the wet to break. As we were reading books in his study, a tall skinny man with a tight-cropped flat-top, white short-sleeved shirt, and black rimmed eyeglasses, burst into Daddy's office. We recognized him immediately. It was

Cammie's daddy. He was a boss at *Brook's Brothers* grocery store. My brother and I had often turned in cold-drink deposit bottles at his store; we'd collect them around town for picture show money.

One time, we told our younger neighbor boys that they could get a deposit on the brown beer bottles people tossed out. They spent a whole day filling up their *Western Flyer* red wagon, from the Western Auto store on the town square, picking those things up. When they went to cash them in, we could only imagine what had happened. But later that evening, the green, pine cone ambush and epic dirt-clod fight, initiated by those boys, gave us an indication of their success.

Cammie's daddy seemed to be a fairly nice man. He always greeted us pleasantly. Other than our fear of him finding out that it was us who had water-bombed him in his passing Mustang last Halloween, from the flat rooftop of the church fellowship hall, we liked him. Bull Tillis had masterminded that one.

The man's face was red and angry. He acted nothing like neither the deacon he was at the Baptist church, nor the friendly store-keep.

"I want you to do something about those nig…" He abruptly halted his speech when he saw us reading on the floor before continuing, "Those Negro boys swimming in the pool at night. I want that water drained to get rid of all that filth they bring in. My daughter is not gonna swim in that."

I didn't know what was going on. We all became uncomfortable at his loud tone.

"I have a daughter, too," my father interjected.

"Well, that's fine for you. You aren't much different than the color'ds themselves. Just got lighter skin," he shouted. "Now drain that filthy water!"

My father spoke directly to him with firm eye contact. He didn't seem to be afraid, but rather irritated by the disposition of the belligerent man. Daddy's speech was calm but unambiguous. He told the man that he would not be draining the pool. He also added that he filtered the water every night after the children swam.

"Then I want extra chlorine added to the water. And if you won't take care of this problem over there, I have a few friends who will!" With that being said, the man with the throbbing veins in his bright red neck and face, turned and left as abruptly as he had burst in.

My father plopped into his chair. He gazed at us and smiled. We were puzzled but felt at ease by my daddy's gesture. It was comforting.

The next day, the water stung our eyes as we swam. No matter how much Cindy, Cammie, and the rest of us complained to Ryan and Peggy about it, the conditions lasted for several more days before returning to normal.

Saturdays were a big deal in our little town. Everybody came to the square and surrounding businesses to visit and shop. It was the center point of the municipality. A large courthouse sat in the middle of it. For my brother and me, Saturday was a day to go to the Show.

We hardly ever missed a matinee; unless of course, it was something other than biker shows and horror movies. But Mr. Henny, the Palace Theater's owner, kept us and the rest of the town's young men in full fodder with these genres at his picture house. Often, it was a two for one. That really stretched our fifty cents admission price. Even if it wasn't a double feature, we could still stay and watch it again at no extra charge.

Today was a real treat. It was a repeat of one of our favorites—*Chamber of Horrors*. It contained one of the best scenes ever filmed. A man actually cut his own hand off to escape prison, and then got an Oriental guy to create sinister attachments so he could wreak all sorts of terror.

The movie also had a unique feature *never before seen*. We speculated it was for the girls. They called it the *Fear Flasher* and the *Horror Horn*. Explained at the beginning of movie, the narrator said that at the start of a scary scene, the screen would flash red and a horn sound would blare. We didn't need a warning, but the visual queue did peak our interest in what havoc was about to happen.

Once we stepped into the show, we saw Lincoln, Ray Ray, and Rabbit at the concession counter.

"Hey y'all," I greeted.

"Hey," they said.

We exchanged soul brother handshakes. "Solid," we said.

Then we got our SOS drinks which were a mixture of every cold drink on tap, and ordered a box of Junior Mints. The four of us started to leave the lobby area when Mrs. Henny called out from behind us—"You colored boys make sure y'all go up in the balcony."

"Yes Ma'am," Lincoln and Rabbit replied.

Once we had gotten to the side steps by the upstairs passage, Rabbit said "Hey, y'all wanna sat wit us?"

We had never been up in the balcony before. It usually had rope with a CLOSED sign on it. And for some reason, our folks always told us that we couldn't go up there. They didn't say *don't* go up there; they just said we *couldn't* go up there. Since the rope was down, and Lincoln and Rabbit were going, I said, "Okay." And we did.

The balcony looked much the same as the downstairs. The only thing different about it was that the seats were smooth, wooden, fold-downs like the ones in our old school gym. They didn't have the cushioned, fuzzy fabric like those downstairs. And it was darker.

But upon further inspection, I found the most amazing thing to be true. The view was great! We could see everything from up here. And I surmised that when we threw popcorn or ice at the ladies titties on the screen, that not only would it travel farther, but that we were most likely less apt to get caught doing it. That made everyone giddy.

The show started out as any other with the same old previews. Mr. Henny played a lot of repeated movies at matinee time. But one preview stood out enough for us to take notice. It was a brand new chopper movie that was *Coming Soon*, it said.

Lincoln and Rabbit got very excited when the narrator said that Marvin Gaye was going to be in it. I knew Marvin Gaye. Ryan played his music at the pool to impress Peggy. That announcement didn't do much for me but the army men and the choppers did. We had missed out on *Easy Rider*, the most famous of all the chopper movies, because it was rated R. But *Chrome and Hot Leather* was rated GP, so we could go see it.

We all were very excited about the prospect of the seeing the new biker movie. Rabbit was talking about the time he saw *Easy Rider*, but we knew he was a *lie*. He just kept repeating the scenes we had all seen on the previews. And when we pressed him about the rest of the movie, he just fumbled around and came up with some obvious stuff that just didn't match up. He wasn't a very good liar.

At that moment Rabbit, Lincoln, and I all decided that we would make our bikes into choppers. We went on so elaborately about it that we missed half of the horror show we had come to see. Only when the screen flashed red and the horror horn blasted did we indulge ourselves in the muted gore of glorious frightfulness. The show was over before we knew it.

Still beaming with excitement over the previews of *Chrome and Hot Leather*, I decided to walk with Lincoln to the feed store so he could meet up with his family. Rabbit had plans to go somewhere else. Our long forgotten little brothers tagged along. For some reason they seemed relieved that we had decided not to stay for the second showing.

On our way to meet up with Lincoln's folks, I stopped in at the Rexall drugs. They had the best selection of comic books in town.

"Lincoln. Y'all gonna come in and get a new *Sgt. Rock* or *Eerie*?"

He stopped at the doorway and looked in. A man inside glared at us sternly from behind the glass entrance.

"Naw. I don't think so. I'll just go on to the Lone Star. I'll see ya' there."

With that we parted and agreed to meet up in a few minutes. I pulled open the heavy, tempered, glass door. A rush of cold air bathed my brother and me as we stepped up onto the elevated landing and went inside. The temperature change was refreshing. But the odd mixed smells of rubbing alcohol, medicines being compounded, and brown gravy—made my stomach a little queasy.

The comic book rack was located near the lunch counter and the cash register. We went directly to it in anticipation of savoring the delights of what we might find there. Several new issues had arrived. Neither of us could wait to get started choosing the perfect one.

"You boys ought keep bedda cump'ny," an older man in overalls said from the counter.

At first I didn't know he was talking to us. But a younger man with the same clothing style and a hat sitting next to him said "Ain't you that Meth'dist preacher's boys?"

I turned and saw the unshaven faces of two men. They looked like farmers. They had on the same type of clothes my grandfather wore. But their faces were less kind than his. I felt uneasy.

"Yes sir," I replied, and I quickly grabbed two *Eerie* magazines from the rack. I tugged at my little brother's arm and told him we needed to go. He wasn't happy about it, but he relented.

We paid a portly, red-haired lady at the register for our comics and started to walk out of the door. The two men and another said something to us that I could not completely hear. They snickered as we left. I had never seen them before, but I was sure I didn't want to again.

The Lone Star feed store was only a few blocks from the square. It was in the direction of "the quarters" and the dump on the way out of town. I never really knew why it was called *the quarters*, I just knew Lincoln and them lived out that way.

The air became thick and smoky as we got closer to our destination. It was the nectarous aroma of barbeque. There were several pickup trucks parked on the front side of the building. Music and loud voices came from the back area.

"Hey, Mr. Russell," I shouted as our feet creaked on old, worn boards upon our entrance. The interior of the place had a much more pleasing aroma than the drug store. It was sweet smelling like molasses and fertilizer. A light, white-grey dust covered almost everything; the same dust that was in Grandpa's feed barn. The store was packed with merchandise of every agricultural necessity. We liked to come in and just look around. In the spring, he had baby chicks and ducklings.

"How you boys?" Mr. Russell returned. "Looking forward to pecan season?"

"Yes sir," I said directly. "Can't wait." He chuckled at that.

Mr. Russell bought pecans. Many a child would pick up the nuts from every corner of town. Sometimes the gleaning would irritate folks. You always had to ask the owner of the property if they minded that you picked up pecans in their yard. Sometimes they didn't care and they would split the difference of the bounty with you. Other times, they would run a picker off with a broom or threaten to tell your mama if they thought their hoard was being stolen.

Pecans were a big deal in East Texas. And Mr. Russell paid a pretty penny for a sack of the native nuts. It was a wage worth the price of comic books, and admission to picture shows many times over. Plus, a paper sackful paid better than the deposits on cold drink bottles; especially the dirty, old, brown ones worth nothing—as our neighbor boys had found out.

"Hey Lincoln!" I shouted from the rear docks and into the gravel back-lot. "I got us a new *Eerie* with a birdman monster and a caveman on it!"

"Awwwww, solid brotha!" he called back as I held it high into the air. I could tell he was as pleased I was.

Lincoln met my brother and me at the bottom of the loading dock steps. I handed him the magazine and we immediately began to thumb through it. We pointed out our favorite pictures to each other. My brother also commented on his new *Fantastic Four* featuring *Hulk vs. Thing*.

"My cousin's over here playin' with Lightnin' today. Let's go wa'ch 'em," my friend said as he led us to a big, shady Hackberry tree. We went to the far backside of the feed store building. Lincoln's cousin was a blues guitarist. I didn't know who Lightnin' was, but a very large group of people had gathered to hear them play.

From time to time, some of the elder folks kept saying that they remembered when the older guitarist would play here at the Lone Star. They said he was much younger then; that is when Mr. Russell's daddy was alive. I didn't know anything about that, but I did like to come and listen to the music and eat smoked, beef sausage served on a slice of white bread. The wurst was almost like that from the Czech butcher shop at Grandpa's. And Mr. Russell's bottles of Big Red soda water were ice cold.

Sometimes Ryan would be here if he didn't have to work at the pool. Given the larger than usual crowd that had started to form, I expected this man was someone he would have wanted want to see. But, I didn't see him. Most everyone except us was what Gran had told me to say were *black folks*.

Nevertheless, we felt right at home as usual with our friends.

"Hey Lincoln, isn't that Mae Annie?"

He looked over to where I was pointing with my sausage in hand.

"Yeah," he said without any further discourse.

"Well, where's she been? I haven't seen her since the fifth grade?" I inquired.

Mae Annie was wearing a plain thin and dirt-stained cotton dress. She was helping two men stack burlap feed bags onto the back of an old flat bed pickup. It was rusty brown and looked like something we played in when we went fishing with Bull Tillis at the pond. When we got tired of fishing, we would play bank robbers in an abandoned truck out there. Bull always brought Swisher Sweet cigars to smoke and Nips breath drops for when we went home. It amazed me that the old truck my schoolmate was loading could even run.

"She stays at home with her Pops," Lincoln replied to my question. "Her mama took sick and died last year. Two white men that have a place next to Mae Annie's did somethin' to her mama. Rabbit's brother said they hurt her some kinda way. Her daddy's been keeping her close ta' home ever since. I saw those men at the Rexall."

"Well, did her daddy call the po'leece?"

"Naw, man. The po'leece ain' gonna do nuthin' to 'em. Rabbit's brothers and his friends said they would git 'um sometime."

I wished that Mr. McConnell would have known about this. He would be able to help. He was a good lawyer, my folks said. He could help out.

I felt bad for Mae Annie. I always had felt bad for her. In the fifth grade, just after we moved here, we were in class together. We had a teacher named Mrs. Walker. She did not like Mae Annie.

I guess Mae Annie didn't have any water in her house. She never seemed to take a bath. Every time she came to school, Mrs. Walker would spray some really awful smelling deodorant spray all around where Mae Annie was sitting. It would make all of us cough. Then she would shout at her, "Go to the nurse and take a shower." It always embarrassed her. Some kids would laugh. I always felt embarrassed too, but probably not as much as my friend. We usually sat next to each other in class. Mae Annie was absent a lot during that grade. Towards the end of the school year I never saw her again, until today.

Mae Annie's thin, cotton dress showed her tall, slender body almost naked in the sunlight. When she sat down on the feed sacks in the back of the truck, I waved at her. Her daddy saw me waving and he said something angry to her. She didn't wave back. Our eyes just locked as they drove away from the docks. My friend held on tightly to the sacks in the open bed as the noise of the dilapidated machine rumbled away in the dust. She looked sad.

We were all having a good time at the barbeque listening to the music. Ray Ray and my brother were looking over his new comic book. Lincoln and I were trying to avoid Bertha Carey, who had shown up—or at least I was.

But during the festivities, a commotion ensued. There had been a fight over by the docks. All I could see was some man slumped against a truck, and some other men on top of another man holding him down. They punched him from time to time until the Sheriff came. The music stopped. People started to wander away from where Lincoln's cousin had been playing. Some older folks told us to stay where we were. We couldn't see much of anything else.

Several minutes later, Uncle Red came over to where we were sitting with Lincoln's family. He told Lincoln's mama that Rabbit's older brother had been in a fight *with a white man*. He said the white man had been stabbed in the belly. Another of Rabbit's brother's friends had slashed the man's face. Rabbit's brother had been caught, but the other boy had gotten away.

Lincoln whispered to me, "It's that white man I saw at the Rexall."

The thought made me scared. *What was going on?*

———————

A couple of weeks later, Mama announced we would not be going to church at the Methodist's today. My brother and I were thrilled. But then she said, "We are going to Miss Flo's church. With Mrs. McConnell and her girls."

The announcement was met with mixed emotions. First, we did not have to sit and hear Daddy preach another long winded sermon today. And for that matter we assumed we didn't have to face Miss Cappadocia Crell for another one of her boring Sunday school lessons either. On the other hand it did appear we had to go to church of some sort. But hopefully it would be more exciting than the one we usually attended. I failed to imagine how this would be of good consequence though.

Secondly, we were going with Mrs. McConnell. Ordinarily this would not be a concern. However, there was the matter of an incident from a few weeks back that I am sure was not totally resolved between us.

Early in June, we and two of the McConnell girls were sitting in the balcony during church. My sister and their youngest were about the same age so they had to sit downstairs with Mama. The middle sister was a year younger than my brother and the oldest was his age. I was older than the rest. Because I was the eldest and given the task to watch out for my brother and the two older girls, we were all allowed to sit up there. The only other people ever to sit in the church balcony sometimes were the senior youth group kids. On this occasion it was just the four of us.

This was only the second or third time we had been allowed to sit upstairs. I can't say who it was, but I am sure it was one of the McConnell girls who did it.

We used to make paper airplanes with our bulletins. Unfortunately, one of them found its way over the railing. It slowly and gracefully drifted over the congregation below, before taking a nose dive into Mr. Saul's bald head. He always sat in the middle row to our left.

Luckily for us, my father didn't see it. He was so engrossed with preaching that he had not a clue. My mother had been tending to my little sister and the youngest McConnell child on the back pew. The balcony hung slightly over the back benches, so she was oblivious as well. But not Mrs. McConnell—she sat in the choir behind my father.

The choir section was staggered behind the pulpit and had a perfect line of sight facing the congregation. While everyone else was asleep listening to my father ramble on, Mrs. McConnell eyed us like a Red-tailed Hawk. And she had seen it all.

The most unfortunate part about the incident was that the McConnell girls got *whoopins*. Unfortunate for them, but not us; my brother and I pleaded ignorance and innocence. But the heavy cost of being banned from the balcony for a month, and the ever gazing stink eye from Mrs. McConnell was often too much to bear. I was getting over it though.

The small, white clapboard church that Miss Flo attended had a sandy parking lot and an outside pavilion. When we went inside, it smelled like any other church—old wood and books. The foyer had a picture of Jesus like the one in our church. But this Jesus had darker skin. He still had *good hair* like Uncle Red, but he looked a lot darker than the one in our sanctuary's vestibule.

There also was picture of a president we studied in school—John F. Kennedy. He looked the same color as usual. And there was another picture of Dr. somebody. He must have been an important man because not only was he a doctor, but a king as well.

"How y'all doin'?" Miss Flo greeted. "Come on in and sit with me and my daughter up front."

Miss Florentine had the fanciest hat I had ever seen. As a matter of fact, all the ladies in the church were sporting fancy hats. Hardly any lady in our church wore anything like that and none as fine as any of these ladies wore. I felt like something festive was about to take place.

When we were handed bulletins, I hoped that there wasn't a balcony. But when we were given fans—I became excited. They had a picture of two pretty little girls praying on the front that read *Thank You God*. On the back it had an address for a funeral home and read, *A new modern funeral home for your comfort*. I wasn't sure if we were coming to a funeral or church service, but I knew it was going to be a special day.

Miss Flo escorted us to a reserved pew upfront. I now knew for sure that there would be no acting up. Lincoln and Ray Ray were sitting behind us. Upon realizing that my brother and I were sitting with a bunch of girls, Miss Flo asked Lincoln's mama if they could sit with us. Miss Florentine was nice like that. Their mama agreed and we squeezed in at the end. All of us boys were grateful to have the same gendered company.

The service began with a greeting from Mr. Preacher. He said something about being glad Mama and Mrs. McConnell had come, and asked if there were any other visitors. He then said, "We welcome you all to the Emmanuel African Methodist Episcopal Church. Amen!"

And the congregation said, "Amen!"

Right away I noted the word *Methodist*. We were Methodist. And perhaps these folks were Czech, too, I considered.

The church service started like any other my father had directed. There were hymns, announcements, and scripture readings. The choir seemed to be a lot happier though. And the people sang with more energy. They actually acted like they wanted to be there. Folks would sway and clap and shout out sometimes. Lincoln and I sat drawing choppers on our bulletins.

Then came the offering—in fact, there were two. The first, Mr. Preacher said, was for *widows and orphans*. Folks would get up, go to the altar table, and place the gifts in a straw basket. There was nothing unusual to me about that. But the second offering was. I had never heard of a second offering.

"Now rise everyone and we shall give gifts and prayers to the Lord. Please stand and turn to the back of the church. You will be escorted to the front to offer your tithes and concerns. Jesus loves a cheerful giver. Amen!"

Everyone answered in the same exuberant fashion. When our backs had been turned, the special-offering music commenced. The choir began to sing, the people started to sway and clap, and the seats emptied from the back of the church to the front—pew by pew.

"Why is everybody turned backwards?" I asked Lincoln.

"That's because no one can see what you're givin'," he said.

When we got to the altar, two silver collection plates were starting to overflow with cash and folded up papers. I put in the nickel that Mama had given me. I saw Mrs. McConnell and Miss Flo putting in money and creased notes before being ushered along.

The papers were curious to me. Also odd was the fact that the choir was turned toward the wall singing, and Mr. Preacher was turned backwards, too. Only two men stood beside the altar table and they faced the wall as well. But perhaps the most curious thing was seeing what looked like Rickie Strange singing lead in front of the choir.

When everyone had finished, we were all directed to turn back and sit down. Indeed, I knew the face staring back at me from the choir. It was Rickie Strange and her crazy eye. She looked happy to see me. I couldn't say I felt the same and wondered when her partner was going to show up.

"We are going to have some special music now," Mr. Preacher announced. "Miss Rickie is gonna sing us an old spiritual with the choir. *Gonna shout all over God's heaven*."

I was surprised at how well Rickie sang. I never even thought about her singing anything. But there she was—keeping time with the piano and everything. She sounded good.

Some of the words made me ponder.

I've got shoes, you've got a shoes
All of God's children got shoes
When I get to Heaven goin' to put on my

This made me think back to Mae Annie. She always wore shoes from the dump. Sometimes they would be tattered and worn, and sometimes they would be some they had made themselves. I remember a pair of sandals she made once. The soles were old tires and the straps were bailing twine; I prayed that she would get some new shoes when she went to heaven.

After the singing, Mr. Preacher began to talk again. I was already wondering when church was going to be over. It was exciting and different, but I was about ready to go. Lincoln and I had filled up our bulletins with drawings. Then he called to Mrs. McConnell and introduced her to the congregation.

"We are so honored to have a special guest with us today. Y'all all know Mr. Aubrey McConnell has been assigned to represent Clarence in this time of need. Well, since he could not be here today, Mrs. McConnell has come to bring words of encouragement and a message for our community."

Mrs. McConnell went on to speak about things I did not understand. She also spoke about a doctor that was a king. I think she may have been referring to the man whose picture was in the foyer. She apologized that Mr. McConnell was not there, saying something about him not being allowed to for some kind of law or something. Many people listened intently. Lincoln and I just kept drawing until folks stood up and started saying *Thank You and Amen*. I thought it was time to go. But I was wrong.

I found out that Mr. Preacher was even more long winded than my father in the pulpit. He just kept on talking. He did make it lively though. I don't think anyone fell asleep there like folks did in our church. He had everyone shouting, *I got a crown!* I liked that. I shouted too.

When I looked around, even Miss Arthur seemed to stay awake. I had espied her earlier, sitting in the pews a few rows behind us. She looked miserable because her blue dress was so tight that no one could have stuffed another piece of her into it. But her huge, fancy, feathered hat did make her look smaller than normal. Although, apparently those Ayds candies still weren't working for her.

In the end, Mr. Preacher finished up and we sang a couple more hymns. I was sure we could go home now. It seemed as if the pool would be closed by the time we got there. But it wasn't to be. Mama said they were having lunch and it would be rude for us to leave early. By this time I was starving and didn't push the issue.

When we reached the outside, several men had already been setting up the pavilion. I was wondering whose barbeque it was outside. For at least the past hour the smell of grilled meat had wafted about the sanctuary. It was not just some neighbor, it was for the church. And we all were very grateful.

The experience at Lincoln's church was a fun one. We had gotten to play together after the service and of course Rickie had tagged along irritating us. Ray Ray and my brother played a few games of marbles with some other boys in the sandy parking lot. But my friend and I mostly discussed how our bike designs for the choppers were coming along.

Lincoln said that he and Rabbit had made a deal with Uncle Red to help them.

They would have to work in his mechanic shop for the rest of the summer to pay off their expenses for the manufactured forks. I said that my father was going to take us to the dump to look for a design he had thought up. We were all very happy that the projects were taking shape.

The day grew long. Folks started to conclude their visiting. The tables were cleared and leftovers were divided up. Because the pool closed early on Sunday's, we didn't make it back in time to swim.

So it was that my father, brother and I found ourselves traveling back down Lee Street to the dump. We passed Mr. Russell's feed store where the fight had occurred. Then we started out of town and passed the old Cotton Gin #3 that we were forbidden to play in, but sometimes sneaked a peek inside of. As we started to reach the quarters, I still wondered about the name. To me it sounded like money. But this part of town didn't seem like it had much of that.

Most of the houses were older. Mama said they were shotgun style. That got my imagination going. There were nice houses with pretty yards, but none were as fancy and large as the Baptist preacher's house down the street from us. Not even our parsonage was as big as that. Still, the houses in our part of town were larger than most of these. And they seemed to be so far away from town. It would be a long walk just to get to the square from here, I thought.

As we passed by Lincoln and Miss Flo's church, I pointed it out to my father. He said he knew of it, and Mr. Preacher. But he called Mr. Preacher *Pastor Jenkins*. I had never heard that before. Everyone else just called him Preacher. I thought I better add the mister part, because that is was what Rabbit and them called a white boy who was nicknamed *Preacher*, too. They also called that boy *white trash*, so I don't think they liked him much. Most folks called my father Pastor.

Actually, the preacher and pastor thing was at times confusing. People in my church called my father *pastor*. People in the Baptist church called their pastor *preacher*. Sometimes people at churches called some men *brother*. And on the street, the name was so mixed up calling ministers one thing or another or both, that I just couldn't keep up with any of it. All I knew was that they all called us *the preacher's kids*. Sometimes people would scowl when they said that. I didn't know why.

The dump was not far from the quarters. We finally pulled in with our big, white, Ford station wagon. Daddy parked at the pit area where the old refrigerators were. He grabbed his hack saw, and my brother and I got out.

"Well, let's look around. We want an old bike," my father said.

There was all kind of junk. We even saw a beat up Coke machine that reminded me of the one we had back at the Houston church. The pit was not that big, but it was full. After a few minutes, my father spotted something he liked.

"Look at that one!" he exclaimed, pointing to a big blue and white granny bike with a basket.

"No, Daddy! I don't want that thing!" I was perturbed. My brother laughed.

"We don't want the whole bike. We just need to cut the forks off and slide them over your old ones to make it longer in front. They need to be big enough," he stated as he made his way over to the atrocious looking dinosaur.

As my father began to saw apart the front of the bike, I began to feel relieved. The wheel was missing and it didn't take him long to finish the job. When he came out of the pit, he smiled broadly with two long stems that curved slightly.

"Here, now all we have to do is trim these up and slide them over your old forks. The ends are wide enough from that old bike, so it should work perfectly."

My father seemed to be quite pleased with himself. I was glad he had the insight to make it happen—until my brother spoke up.

"You're gonna have a granny chopper."

I threw a punch but missed as he ducked away and ran off. My father yelled at us and we went back to the car. Despite my brother's comment, I was eager to get home and build my chopper so I could show it off at the pool.

As my father was putting the acquired metal into the vehicle, Mr. Preacher pulled up next to us.

"Hello there, Pastor Jenkins," my father greeted.

"Hello there y'self, Pastor," the man chuckled.

"Want some help with that 'ol washer?" Daddy asked.

Great I thought. *I gotta wait on these two now.*

The two men unloaded a rust blotched machine and pushed it into the pit. It clanged against the paint chipped red and white Coke machine. They then entered into conversation, not all of which I heard from my rolled-down window seat of the hot car.

"I appreciate your wife and children coming to service the other day."

"They had a good time. I wish I could have come to the luncheon, but we had one, too," Daddy said.

"Well, I understand. Preachers always gotta schedule to keep up," Mr. Preacher replied. The two men agreed.

"Anything new with your grandson?" Daddy asked.

"Well, yes'suh, sho' is," the preacher started. "Saw him in the jail. I know Mr. McConnell can't talk about it, but I can. Reckon it's alright since we're preachers. Confidentiality and all."

"Sure, that's true if you need some prayer on it."

"Oh, yessir, we do," Mr. Preacher said. Between you, me, and the Lord."

The two men began to talk a little more hushed, and moved a little father from the car. I could still hear some of the conversation. Some of what I heard, I didn't fully comprehend. They continued their discussion as I tried to grasp the meaning.

Mr. Preacher revealed that Rabbit's brother told him that he had a shallow stab wound to his left side. It was from a pocket knife like a Buck knife. The preacher called it a *pig sticker*. He said that the police had never checked the injured *older white man* for weapons because they found a butterfly knife on the ground that *belonged to Clarence*. They said Clarence had fallen on his own knife. The police did not check the white man for any weapons because they assumed *the colored boy* was the perpetrator.

The butterfly blade was reported to be six inches long; a Buck blade is three and a half inches long. The police noted that a blade went through Clarence's leather jacket and into his side. It penetrated only about two inches.

Three witnesses claimed they saw the two men arguing and that Clarence pulled out a knife and cut the older man. Clarence claimed that he and his friend were walking past a truck on the street side of the parking area, when the older white man stuck him with a knife as they passed by. The pickup truck had blocked the initial view of the incident from the crowd or any other potential witnesses.

Preacher recounted that it was then that the men began to argue. Clarence pulled his knife and stabbed the older man. At some point, Clarence's friend slashed the man's face. A younger white companion to the elder darted from around the backside side of the truck, and sucker punched Clarence's friend knocking him down. Then, the younger man jumped on Clarence as the fight spilled to the front of the vehicle. When two white workers on the dock heard the commotion, they jumped down and helped to subdue Clarence.

The police and the witnesses claimed that Clarence fell on his butterfly knife in the fall. Clarence's friend ran off when the two white workers came running around to the front of truck.

"Mmmh," Daddy said.

"Well, I want y'all to know how much our community appreciates what you have tried to do for us," Mr. Preacher said. "I heard something about Mr. McConnell had some trouble at this office in town the other day."

"Well, yes sir. Guess some folks didn't like him being appointed to defend Clarence. He told the judge he would take the case without bias. The other morning…well, he came to work and someone had white washed *N Lover* on his windows," Daddy said.

"And I'm sure they spelled it out, too, Pastor," Mr. Preacher said.

"Well, yessir, they did. But he got it taken down pretty quick. I think he might have expected some of these less-than-desirable folk would do something like that."

"How 'bout you, sir, any trouble for yo' family?"

"Not really," Daddy stated. "Couple weeks ago had a visitor to my study at the church. Man came in angry because some of the black kids were swimming in the pool at night."

"Aah, yes. I know a few who have. I told them not to do that. If anyone gets hurt swimin' it could make a big problem. Especially if they can't get back out."

"Yessir, but they need to have a place to swim. Desegregation allows everyone the right to swim. Problem is that even though the pool is in the city park, it is still considered a private entity—because the business social clubs run it. And they can make up their own membership rules. It's not right, but they do," Daddy continued.

"Mmmh," Mr. Preacher grunted.

"You know, a few of us brought this up. But the response was that they would rather close it down before they let a…well, before they would open it up to everyone."

"I surely understand. And I'll bet my bottom dolla' that fellow who came to your office was one of the club members against y'all."

"Well, sir, yes he was," my daddy said.

"You can't do much with those folks. Just kinda gotta let things play out. We have those in our community, too. Clarence is one of 'em. Now, it's gonna cost him. Just can't go around talkin' revolution and expect things to change with the white folk right off. Dr. King's way is better," Mr. Preacher said.

"I agree, Pastor. Seems like it's trying to get better, but only prayer will heal."

"Amen, brother. Amen," Mr. Preacher said.

The two men exchanged a few more pleasantries before shaking hands and returning to their respective vehicles.

On the way home, I thought about much of what I had overheard. I wondered if I should continue to ask my father for Lincoln's swim pass. There were things that still confused me, but also things that were starting to become clearer. I didn't quite fully understand it.

The ride back seemed to pass quickly. I contemplated my experiences over the now closing summer. My father and brother were engaged in more conversation due to my chatty absence. The flux of the season's activity seemed to have changed me in some respects. But I could not have possibly known how much just yet.

Only a couple days more and my father had completed my new chopper. The purple bike had been fitted with two, curved front, forks cut from the old dump bike. Although they were blue and the colors did not match exactly, I was elated.

He had also redesigned the ride. By drilling holes into the back seat support and replacing the bolts, he lowered my banana seat down at a backward angle to make a small sissy bar. The antler handlebars were repositioned to a forty-five degree pitch for me to comfortably reach. With the new extended forks, it made my new chopper ride longer and lower to the ground. *It was the most stone cold coolest bike in town.* I could not wait to show Lincoln and Rabbit.

I had long been envious of my brother's bicycle. He had gotten a green Huffy for Christmas two years before. It had a sissy bar taller than he was. But my father said with that with that style of bar, there was no way he could put forks on it, reshape it, and have a safe ride.

My old, off-brand Zebra bike was really shining as a Phoenician goddess now. I basked in the glory of her new ride on the way to the pool. My brother tagged along. Now, it was his turn to be jealous.

As we rode through the park, I looked for my friend. I did not see Lincoln at any of the ball fields or picnic tables. There were not as many people there for a normal Saturday afternoon. I wondered where he was, but never found him. My brother had gone on to swim. After a few rounds through the park, I went on as well.

More children than ever were in the water when I arrived. The August sun was especially hot on this day. Sitting on towels in their usual spot, the Lemon Sisters baked themselves in the heat slathered with baby oil. Contrasting in skin tone, their hair was now much lighter than at the start of the summer. It also looked thinner. There was no telling how much they had lost due to their vain beauty treatment.

One thing for sure was that Cammie's daddy had spent plenty of money on the yellow citrus. But the two brunettes hadn't achieved the natural beauty of Peggy's golden locks. Ryan could attest to that. Yet no matter how much Marvin Gaye he played, she still seemed to keep him at bay. I was much more fortunate.

I found Peggy in her usual spot on the concession counter surveying the pool. The shade inside was cool and the concrete floor felt good on my bare feet. As I climbed up to greet her, it seemed as if less effort was required. Perhaps I had grown a few inches taller.

I seated myself next to her. Again, I was tantalized; ever the opportunist—I relished the beads of sweat upon her breasts. They were especially lovely in her red gingham bikini-top.

"Watchin' the birds, Peggy?" I asked coyly.

"Yes," she said staring outward from her large, brown, tinted sunglasses. "You know, they had a nest up in that ol' oak tree over by the baby pool. And another bird had one in the Horse Apple tree."

"Are they still there?"

"No, they flew away. When they got big. The young males flew from the tree, and over the fence. I never saw them again," she stated matter of factually.

I wondered how she knew that they were boy birds, but then she *was* in college. I just said "Oh."

Peggy and I sat for a long time on that counter. I knew she would be going back to school soon and so would I. It felt good to be close to her. Her skin was now a golden brown. I could see the tan lines around her bikini bottom. Most everyone at the pool had lighter skin underneath their suits.

I had at least two colors of skin—kind of like a Mockingbird. But the notion of being a *colored person* was starting to fade as I thought about what had occurred over the summer.

It seemed lines were drawn by others to define us. Just like the line between Peggy and me. She was older and my chances of ever seeing her naked like Bertha Carey were slim. I felt sure she would never pull her top off and jiggle her grapefruits at me. I could only fantasize about fully seeing her pink nipples and white breasts cloaked by her golden hair. And, I'd never be her boyfriend.

When Ryan came to work later in the day, I decided to go swimming. I knew he wanted to have some time with her. Maybe he would have better luck. Maybe one of us would have their fantasy fulfilled.

The water was cool and it soothed my mind. Cindy Heard and Cammie Scott were being splashed by Bull Tillis. Cynthia Roe entertained the older boys as she smacked against the low dive in one of her famous butt busters. My brother was diving for lost change in the deep end with a friend of his.

I just floated in the shallow water and closed my eyes; the red-orange sun shown through my lids as if a sunrise were glaring. There was an echoic tunnel noise that sounded in my sunken ears. Cool drops of splashed water spray across my red hot face.

I opened my eyes again after several blissful moments. Once they had adjusted back to the brightness, I saw Lincoln and Ray Ray at the fence staring back at me. I had floated full-body-frontal toward their direction. There is no telling how long they had been standing there watching me. I popped up immediately, happy to see them.

"Hey Lincoln!" I shouted from my luxurious, watery spa. Ray Ray waved at me from across the way behind the fence.

I swam as fast as I could to get out of the pool. Part of the way I struggled through impeding water, as I tried to run against its weight while reaching for the ladder. It tired me. When I exited, a great gush of chlorinated ablution came with me onto the burning hot concrete. It temporarily soothed my blistering feet just as the cold, shaded floor in the concession stand had. But full relief was not felt until I reached the benevolent grass by the fence where Lincoln and Ray Ray were standing.

My friend was straddling his bike. His brother had gotten off and was poised behind it at the galvanized barrier. They both looked hot and miserable. Their dark skin glistened in the stark light. Lincoln had beads of sweat on his brow. His short afro reflected what looked to me like the morning dew captured on tiny spider webs in a spring farm pasture. His long, thin fingers clasp through the chain link fence between us.

"Hey Man!" I exclaimed as I put my hand up for a fist bump through the fence. His response was weak at best. No reply of *solid* was given.

"You didn't get your bike done yet?" I asked.

"Naw. Rabbit's is done. Uncle Red welded some forks onto it. He's supposed to do mine next week before we go back to school," he said stoically.

"Oh. Well my dad helped me get mine done. Wanna see it?"

Lincoln said nothing. He just looked right past me and into the pool. Something was not right. He looked sad. Maybe even a bit angry. Either way, he was despondent for sure.

"Hey. I've been trying to get my dad to get y'all some passes so y'all can swim."

I had hoped this statement would cheer him up. But he looked at me blankly. Then his face contorted in a sorrowful way.

"Maaaaan, we ain't never gonna git ta' come inside that fence—'cause we black and you white."

I looked at my friend with befuddled confusion. It was the first time I had ascertained the two words put together like that. Those words were fixated on me. And my best of friends had said it with conviction.

There was a pause—a pause so quiet that no Mockingbird sang and no child's splash could be heard. Our eyes locked intensely. Not angrily, but mournfully. And then tears welled up in my friend's eyes. It was as if he were saying good-bye.

Lincoln turned the front wheel of his bike away from the fence that separated us. He spit on the ground and said to his little brother, "Come on...let's go."

Ray Ray got back on. They rode off into the park as my fingers gripped tightly between the chain links. The restricting grey steel maze obstructed my view. The little boy briefly turned, and then waved with his small fading hands.

I spun away from the fence. Silence ever engulfed me. It was as if my ears were still submerged, but there was no sound. All the kids were playing in the pool's cool refreshment beneath the blistering August sun. *White kids*—our color now confirmed.

Cammie and Cindy were sucking the juice from lemons they used to bleach their yellow hair. Ryan sat on high in his coveted lifeguard chair with his wild, curly, black, pirate locks dangling in the still air. His reddish-brown *Injun-skin* sported that *retarded looking,* white nose cream upon his face. Bull mutely dashed off of the low diving board in a cannonball fury. His pink pork belly jiggled all the way to the jump.

I was on the inside. I was on the inside of the fence. But I felt trapped—not sheltered. I felt trapped in the lies I had been told. *I wasn't colored. I wasn't any color at all—just white. The kind of white that wasn't even a color at all.* It wasn't even the true color of my skin.

But there was something else. And it made me angry. So angry that when the joyful sounds around me flowed back into my ears, I heard the screams and cries of injustice so loud that I bolted out of that place—and straight to my father's study. But unlike the young Mockingbirds, I first had to circumvent the pool's prison-like fence through a series of closed gates.

I left my shoes, shirt, and little brother behind. Peggy called out to me, but I did not reply to her. I just jumped on my bike and started pumping pedals across town to confront my father.

I tried to make sense of it all. *Why did they lie? Why did our parents keep us so sheltered? To protect us? From what?*

It all came crashing down. I was not a child any longer in my eyes. I realized what Lincoln had known for some time—the world we lived in was either black or white. There were no colors in *colored*. There were no *colored people* as I had imagined as a child in Houston—only different shades of skin and hair. *And Daddy lied to me about the guest passes, too?*

I burst into his church study angry like Cammie's daddy had before.

"Why did y'all lie to me?" I demanded.

My father looked up from behind his desk completely confounded.

"You told me Lincoln and them couldn't swim because they weren't members of the pool. That's a lie. They're black! That's why. Because they're black!"

His face grimaced. Then he turned angry. "Who told you that? Where are you gittin' this from?"

"Lincoln! He told me the truth. He said he was never gonna get to swim because he was black and I was white. I thought we were color'd like him. Just different." Tears streamed down my face. I felt dizzy and exhausted.

My father came over to me and helped me into a chair. He pulled another one up beside me and put his hand on the back of my sunburned neck. Daddy did his best to console me with his touch and a sensitive smile.

"I'm sorry," he said. "Maybe Mama and I have not told y'all enough. We wanted you-all to grow up without prejudice. To learn things on your own and not be influenced by other people. That's one reason we moved to a smaller town."

I listened but I still was angry and upset. The tears started to subside and I sniffled. My father retrieved a crocheted afghan from across the room and put it over my bare skin. It was one that my Sunday school teacher Miss Cappadocia Crell had made for him. It seemed ironic, but it comforted me.

"What do you mean colored? Colored like Lincoln?" my father asked.

"Colored people. I used to think there were people of different colors. A man at church in Houston told Mama one time that we were like the colored people because we were Czech. Then I later realized that people just had different skin colors. Gran said that the colored people used to be called Negroes and now we say Black folk. I thought Mr. Marshall and them at Grandpa's were Czech, too. That's why I thought we were colored folk, too. Because of what that man said to Mama."

My father sat quietly contemplating for a moment before saying, "That would have been Mr. Meiners." He scowled at the name.

I had not often seen my father show distaste for too many people. Sometimes he would frown at the news on television, or on the phone when he said some "ignorant people" had called him or my mother before hanging up on them. But I don't ever recall him glowering at a church member.

"Mr. Meiners was a German man in our old church," my father started. "He did not like us much. He claimed to be a direct descendant of a philosopher and scientist from back in the 1700's. I'm not sure how that was because he also claimed his people came over in the German migration to Texas that started in the 1840's. Those immigrants wanted to set up their own country here— called Adelsverein. Not too far from where Uncle Ben lives. Well, his people would have come over at about the same time as ours did during the Czech and Slovak migration of the 1850's."

"How did they get here?" I asked.

"They had to take a ship. They came through Galveston."

"At the beach?" I perked up.

"Yep, at the beach," my father said. "And then your great grandparents took a wagon with some German immigrants to the Snook area and settled there. They were all farmers. That's why I have always wondered that if Mr. Meiners claims to have been descended from such educated people, he obviously has little intelligence to show for it."

My father stopped a moment and adjusted himself in his chair. "It's not that farmers are dumb. Grandpa never finished the seventh grade. Your age now. But he was a smart man. Just not in the school sense."

"The thing about Mr. Meiners is this," Daddy continued, "he is from a group of people who believe they are superior to others. His ancestor called the Slavic people an inferior race, and ugly. He believed that our people and the Negro people were like the same. They called our people, who are the Slavic peoples, *dirty whites*. And that both Negro and Slavic races were dumb."

"That's not right," I chirped. "I'm not dumb. Lincoln's not dumb."

"You're right, y'all aren't. But some people believe that. Both the Negro people and the Slavic people were slaves at one time. In our country, we have a horrible history of Negroes being brought here and used as slaves. The truth is that most everyone was a slave at one time or another. But some people have been exploited and abused more often it seems. Even Czechoslovakia is under communist slavery now. The Nazis killed many, many Slavs when Hitler was in charge. And the black folks here are still being abused and excluded here in our own town, even though it is illegal. Slavery was supposed to be abolished in the United States in 1863 by President Lincoln. Unfortunately, that wasn't told to the Black folks of Texas until 1865."

"Is Mr. Marshall Grandpa's slave?" I asked quietly.

"No," my father chuckled. "Grandpa and Mr. Marshall help each other bring in their crops. He hires Mr. Marshall and others like him in the community. Many times black folks and immigrant folks stick together. Because of people like Mr. Meiners. Just because our skin is lighter than Lincoln and Pastor Jenkins, we are considered white folks for the most part. Until sometimes our last name gives us away as being from a country of less integrity, some would say. Just like the black folk are still considered to be foreigners from the slave trade, we too are sometimes looked down on because our people are considered to be untrustworthy, too. Many think of us as communists because the Soviet Union has taken over our historical home country. But believe me—the black folks have it much worse than we do here today. I can't say how it is over there for our people."

"Is that why Black folk are treated bad, too? Cause they're from another country?"

"No. Most Black folks from around here are descendants of slaves. But they are American citizens. Just in the United States, there was a thing called segregation. That means they kept black and white folks separated."

"Like at the pool? And at the Ballard's drive-in ice cream?"

"That's right," my father said. "But it's not legal anymore. In 1964 the Civil Rights Act was passed to prevent discrimination against black people. President John F. Kennedy tried to get that law into place, but he was killed for it, some say. LBJ did get it passed though. That is why you see some pictures of JFK in some of the churches like Pastor Jenkins'."

I remembered seeing a former president in the A.M.E. foyer.

"Daddy, why is their Jesus dark skinned and ours light skinned? And who is that king that's a doctor in the picture over there, too?"

My father laughed at that question.

"That picture of Jesus is probably more what Jesus actually looked like. He surely didn't have white skin. But people need to think of Jesus lookin' like more of themselves."

"But what about the king?" I pressed.

Again he smiled before saying, "That is Dr. Martin Luther King, Jr. He was a civil rights leader. There are many, but he and Malcolm X are probably the most well known of that time. Dr. King was a Christian that taught nonviolent resistance to achieve the goal of equal civil rights. Malcolm X was a Muslim that some said taught the opposite—a war on white people, like the Black Panthers, some say. Whether that is true or not, it all makes people nervous. That is one reason why a lot of white folks don't want to give up control of the old ways— power over black folks. That's why every one of those men was killed. Out of fear of losing control over something."

"Are we white, Daddy?"

My father looked at me. I'm not sure he knew what to say or if he was thinking about how to say it, but after a moment he did.

"No one should allow themselves or others to define who they are by the color of skin. It is what you do, what you contribute to the community—the world as a whole for that matter. Act kindly. Carry yourself with an uplifting attitude. That makes a person. We all have the same mental capacity to be great. Don't ever think yourself to be more or less than another. Your purpose and path may be different than someone else's, but it is up to you to pursue it honorably. No matter what you do. Or who you are."

I thought about his words. I thought about the pictures in the churches. I envisioned the Black Panthers, Jesus, Miss Florentine, Peggy, Lincoln, and everything from the summer's holiday. It all seemed to just jumble in my head. But it also seemed to make sense in a strange way. It was kind of like when Gran was explaining things to me. It was an epiphany. And I knew my mind and my body had been changed forever.

Daddy went on to explain how the situation in our town had affected him as well. He, Mama and the McConnell's were only some of the white folks working within cultural boundaries to change things. It took time. But my father assured me that things were slowly changing.

He also said that the pool would most likely remain closed to black kids like Lincoln. Most members of the all-white, business social clubs that owned the pool vowed to keep it segregated. When I asked him why he stayed involved with the group, he said it was like medicine. *You might not like the taste of it, but if taking it does some good to heal you—stick it out for the cure.* It would take years for me to realize that. But his advice gave me the encouragement to hope and to see the world as I always had as a child—a world of color, not just black and white.

———————

I hadn't revisited my old town in several years. In 1974 we had moved away to Dallas. Now I had planned a route through the old place on our way to a large family reunion in Burleson County. Most of my wife's people had passed, but she was always welcomed as one of us. When we reached the old quarters, I realized many of the shotgun houses had been replaced with government housing. Pastor Jenkins church was still there but it had gotten a nice facelift and an expansion of sorts.

I thought of Rickie Carey when I saw the church. We had met up in college at UT Austin. She studied music and I became a teacher. Her best friend was left behind, although we both visited her from time to time. Eventually, I moved to *the Valley* and taught in Weslaco. Most of the Independent School District students there spoke Spanish.

My wife and I stopped at what I thought was the old feed store. It now was a music hall and had a historical marker on it. Not far from the old building and near the ancient Hackberry tree was a bronze statue atop a granite base. It was of a man with big glasses and a hat. He was seated and playing his guitar.

It wasn't until I read the plaque that I realized who I was looking at. It was Lightnin'! Despite being a huge Blues fan, I had no idea that our paths had crossed on Clarence's fateful day all those years ago.

Rabbit's brother had been convicted of murder and sentenced to death at the

Huntsville Prison. His friend never made it to court. A group of farmers said they found his body in the Trinity River not far from town.

I thought about that day while standing there. I remembered that Mr. McConnell had represented Clarence, the revolutionary in black shades and leather jacket. He was just a boy really—a boy who wanted better for his people. A boy, the product of oppression, whose dream of a just society had led him to an ill-fated end.

Mr. McConnell had died soon after the trial from cancer. He passed before we moved to Dallas. Daddy had officiated at the funeral. My father later said that the stress of litigation had hastened his condition. The noble Esquire's career was sullied by the case.

I was in awe that now our small town had a monument to a black man. To me it showed a sign of progress. *Could this town have changed? Or was it just inevitable? After all, our country did elect a mixed race President.*

Moving through the municipality, it looked very decayed and run down. The square was empty and many of the old buildings were boarded up. One had a sign that read *Thanks for Nothing WalMart.* I further inferred the town's demise when I saw that the old Duke and Ayers dime store had been turned into a Habitat for Humanity resale shop.

The only thing in town that actually appeared to still be in working order was the Palace movie theater. It had been remodeled. I was shocked to see them advertising a Saturday double-feature matinee. The Brook's Brothers grocery was also still in use. It had been upgraded, too.

The news was not as good for my old junior high school. Down a few blocks from the place we where would sell cold drink bottles—the large, main school building had been torn down. That original structure had been in existence since the 1930's. It had been built as the high school. I was surprised to see it gone. It once was such a beautiful building inside.

I could remember the large halls with wood floors that echoed throughout. We were instructed to tiptoe quietly through them. I'm not sure why. When someone got paddled, teachers didn't worry so much about the detrimental cacophony that reverberated.

And then I thought about Bertha Carey and Rickie Strange. This was the place where they had cornered me and tormented my soul with those little, bud nee-nees in Miss Arthur's class. Memories of all the kids from school flooded my mind.

Rabbit had been killed in a motorcycle accident in high school. Lincoln became a well known Blues pianist. I wondered how Miss Arthur and the others might be faring. I had been away so long and lost touch with most everyone.

The course to the park was paved with new road. Old outlying cotton gins had been dismantled and only the newer installed truck scales of a by-gone era remained unused—frozen with rust. The shady trees were taller it seemed. The path was just as windy but not as long a trip by car. I traveled the same route as I always had on my chopper via our way to the pool.

We got out and looked around once we arrived. The fence that separated Lincoln and me had been torn down. With its cavity filled in, only an overgrown vacant lot remained. The only trace of the pool that was left was the shell's brick edge—a rectangular outline.

Buildings had been demolished and a cow pasture was visible. Only the Mockingbird's lair and the Horse Apple tree were left in a gravely dirt space between the road and the weedy lot.

At first I wondered if I was even at the right spot. But when I ventured out to the place where the fence had been, I knew. I knew I was there. I could now see clearly the formerly obstructed view from over Lincoln's shoulder. I saw shaded spots where many games of marbles had been played on dirt patches during summer breaks. The park picnic tables—the place where we had celebrated Juneteenth. It was the place where Miss Flo had sheltered us from harm, it not seeming so far away from us now in its quiet sentry.

I had mixed emotions about the pool's demise. On one hand I was sad that my childhood memories of swimming bliss where gone. But I also wept at the remembrance of Lincoln and I being separated in that way. And I was glad that the fence was gone.

I stayed and thought about those days for more than an hour. I just wandered, sat, and remembered. I could hear the voices of children's past lives. And I could hear the cries of injustice as well.

Before my wife and I left to continue our journey on, we stood and listened as the Texas state bird sang his sweet song. It was a Mockingbird. And its song could be heard from the old oak tree which was now not only of gained girth, but much nobler. I wondered how many generations had been born in that tree. I wondered how many had not had to fly over that fence, but just hop across the green space that Peggy watched so intently.

It was a new era. Bertha put her hand on mine. Her cinnamon skin was as smooth and beautiful as when I had first met her. Though, it was older now.

We never returned to that place. I didn't look back from the car window that day as I had before. Before, as when I was a child looking back at my black friends swim in the pool after jumping the fence. I prayed that future families would be able to find peace with each other—to congregate and swim freely. And I prayed that all barriers would one day be removed—just like the one at the pool.

Bibliography

"Juneteenth (General Orders, No.3)," Texas State Library Archives, last modified March 25, 2015, https://www.tsl.texas.gov/ref/abouttx/juneteenth.html.

The Duke Adolphus Frederick of Mecklenburg, "A Land of Giants and Pygmies," The National Geographic April 1912: 368-387.

Elise May Bell Grosvenor, "Safari from Congo to Cairo," The National Geographic December 1954: 721-771

Lewis Carroll, "The Walrus and the Carpenter," in *Through the Looking Glass* (United Kingdom: Macmillan, 1871)

Chamber of Horrors, directed by Hy Averback. 1966. USA: Warner Brothers (theatrical)

Chrome and Hot Leather, directed by Lee Frost. 1971. USA: American International Pictures (theatrical)

Eerie Magazine #34, July 1971

Fantastic Four, *Hulk vs. Thing*, Marvel Comic #112, July 1971

"Songs," Going To Shout All Over God's Heaven, accessed April 10, 2015, www.negrospirituals.com

"Desegregation in Austin," accessed April 10, 2015, http://www.austinlibrary.com/ahc/desegregation/

"Christoph Meiners," Thiel, Udo (2006), "Meiners, Christoph", in Haakonssen, Knud, *The Cambridge History of Eighteenth-Century Philosophy* 2, Cambridge University Press, p. 1203, via Wikipedia, accessed April 10, 2015, https://en.wikipedia.org/wiki/Christoph_Meiners

"Texas State Historical Society," accessed April 10, 2015, https://tshaonline.org/handbook

www.ingramcontent.com/pod-product-compliance
Lightning Source LLC
Chambersburg PA
CBHW020250150626
46552CB00020B/744